# PHEW, WHAT A SCORCHER!

Beth moved herself over onto her tummy and asked Nick if he would put some suntan lotion on her back.

'My pleasure,' he said, reaching out for the bottle. He sat up to unscrew the cap and he poured out a little puddle into the palm of his other hand. But before he could transfer it to Beth's back, she brought round her arms and unclipped the catch of her bikini which she then slipped off and, raising her body so that he caught a fleeting glimpse of her bare breasts, threw the top onto the towel.

'That's better, you can dab some oil on now. I just don't want to have any white lines showing,' she explained.

Nick smoothed the oil onto her warm skin. 'M'mm, what a wonderfully light touch you have,' murmured Beth, but his hands began to tremble when she added: 'but please don't neglect my bottom. The main reason why I agreed to wear this bikini was that I would be able to expose my bum cheeks to the sun . . .'

# SUMMER SCHOOL 1:
## WARM DAYS, HOT NIGHTS

DICK ROGERS

BLUE MOON BOOKS
NEW YORK

*Summer School 1: Warm Days, Hot Nights*
Copyright © 1994, 2005 by Potiphar Productions

Published by
Blue Moon Books
An Imprint of Avalon Publishing Group Incorporated
245 West 17th Street, 11th floor
New York, NY 10011-5300

First Blue Moon Books Edition 2005

First Published in 1994 by Hodder & Stoughton

ISBN 1-56201-468-4

9 8 7 6 5 4 3 2 1

Printed in Canada
Distributed by Publishers Group West

This is for fair Jenny of Hampstead Garden Suburb

On with the dance! let joy be unconfined:
No sleep till morn, when Youth and Pleasure meet
To chase the glowing hours with flying feet.

*Lord Byron*
1788–1824

# CHAPTER ONE

## *Meet the Boys*

A large smile of contentment spread over Nick Armitage's face as he gazed round the plushly decorated restaurant of The Garment District, a small private gentleman's club in Great Titchfield Street which was patronised mostly by young executives in the growing number of rag trade businesses which had recently sprung up behind the busy shopping area in the heart of London's West End.

'Steve, I'm over here,' he called out as he saw his lunch guest, Steven Williams, a BBC radio producer who worked at Broadcasting House just a few minutes' walk away, stroll into the room.

He waved to his old school friend who gave his raincoat to Oscar, the burly restaurant manager, before hurrying across to join Nick at his table.

'Hi there, mate, sorry I'm late, but we were recording *The Afternoon Play* this morning and one of the actresses threw a wobbly.'

An attractive, mini-skirted waitress placed a bottle of champagne in the ice-bucket at the side of their table and Nick winked at the girl. 'Hello, Chrissie, how are you keeping? Any news yet from your agent about the audition you went for last week?'

The girl shook her head and sighed: 'Not a word yet, Mr Armitage. I really thought I was in with a chance but there must have been fifty of us chasing the two parts. I'm keeping my fingers crossed, though, because they say that the film is going to be a sort of sequel to *Blow Up*.'

'Wow! Well, if you do get the part and you and another girl have to roll around on the floor of a photographer's studio whilst David Hemmings pulls off your clothes, I'll book tickets for the premiere right now!' Nick chuckled, but Chrissie wagged a reproving finger at him.

'Oh Nick, you disappoint me!' she said teasingly as she gave menus to the two men. 'There was I thinking that you enjoyed *Blow Up* because of Antonioni's clever questioning of where fantasy meets reality, and it turns out that all you remember were the flashes of nudity.'

'Here, that's not fair,' Nick protested as he glanced down to see if the *table d'hôte* bill of fare was to his liking. 'Sure, I was turned on by Jane Birkin's tits but look, this is 1967 and only down the road in Soho there are more strip clubs than I've had hot dinners.'

Steve gave a short laugh and remarked: 'Maybe so, but you wouldn't want to be seen going into one of those crummy joints.' He gave Chrissie a knowing wink and Nick threw up his hands in mock surrender and said: 'Okay officer, it's a fair cop and I'll come quietly! I dare say that if there hadn't been all the fuss about that two-girl naked romp, I might not have bothered to go and see the bloody film.

'Anyhow, Chrissie, play your cards right today and I'll introduce you to my pal here who's a great contact for an aspiring actress like you. Steve's a radio producer with the BBC. Think of what he could do for your career!'

'I'm not worth the big build-up, love,' Steve said regretfully. 'Ninety-nine times out of a hundred we cast the minor roles from the BBC's own repertory company.'

'But couldn't you arrange an audition for Chrissie with this company?' urged Nick. 'I mean, isn't she a stunner?'

'Without a doubt,' grinned Steve broadly, 'although that would be of limited value for steam radio!'

Chrissie brushed back stray strands of tawny hair from her face. 'I'm not just a silly dollybird, Steve, I've done my stint of Shakespeare at RADA but it's so hard to find work without an Equity card.'

'Equity? That's the actors' trade union, isn't it?' asked Nick.

'Yes, and it's a real Catch-22 situation for newcomers,' said Steve with genuine sympathy. 'You can't get an Equity card till you get work and you can't get work without an Equity card!'

'So what can Chrissie do?' Nick wondered and he was answered by a guttural growl of: 'She can take your order for a start,' from Oscar, the manager of the club restaurant, for the place was filling up and Chrissie had customers on five other tables to serve.

Nick glanced again at the menu and said: 'Today's Special will do me fine – Prawn Cocktail, Rump Steak and Chips and the Sweet Trolley – what about you, mate?'

'I'll have the same,' said Steve and Nick ordered a bottle of the club claret from the wine list before Chrissie whisked the menus away and scurried off back to the kitchen.

'So what's new, Nick?' asked Steve, who had been a close pal of Nick Armitage since their days at Cambridge University which they had left four years ago in the summer of 1963, when the Beatles heralded in the sexual revolution which was transforming the fuddy-duddy British way of life and made Swinging London 'the city of the decade' according to *Time* magazine.

He went on: 'You look well-pleased with life, so I suppose this means that you finally persuaded the lovely Hazel into your bed, you lucky sod!'

'Even better than that, Steve,' replied Nick with a

wolfish grin. 'I not only made it with Hazel last night but also with Mandy, her cousin from Birmingham who I told you about on Thursday. You remember, she's the girl who works at a travel agency and is staying at Hazel's whilst she's in London on one of those freebie trips the tour operators arrange for the travel trade.'

Since their time at Cambridge, Steven Williams had always been impressed – and at times more than a mite envious – of what he called Nick's unremitting pursuit of pussy. During their first days at college, he had seen his extrovert friend make a bee-line for the most appetising eighteen-year-old girl in their class and successfully seduce her after the Freshers' Ball.

He breathed hard and said: 'Go on, then, I can see that you're bursting to tell me all about it. Come on, let's have a blow-by-blow account.'

'There were no blows,' said Nick indignantly. 'I hope I'd never sink so low as to use force in order to have my wicked way. No, old boy, I simply accepted what was freely offered to me by Hazel and Mandy last night. I hadn't expected Hazel to call me and was planning to get through some paper-work when she called and said that it was Mandy's birthday and she'd been given a bottle of champagne by the company which was sponsoring her visit, and would I like to come over and help them drink it?

'Well, it sounded a lot more fun than making up my expenses for the last four weeks, so I had a quick shower, pulled on my new Cecil Gee sweater and was ringing the doorbell at Hazel's flat in less than an hour clutching a bottle of Eau de Cologne from the late night chemist in my hot little hand. Actually I hadn't met Mandy before, but if she was kind enough to ask me to join her birthday party I wanted to buy her a little present.

'Steve, you've met Hazel and you know that she's

4

gorgeous but I'm telling you, mate, one look at Mandy just blew my mind. She's taller than Hazel with long auburn hair that cascaded over her slim shoulders and she was wearing a baby blue angora top which showed off her small but firm-looking tits and a tight mini-skirt which accentuated her beautiful long legs.

'Well, the three of us sat down and chatted whilst we listened to the music of The Beatles, Bob Dylan and the Rolling Stones whilst we drank the champagne – a superb 1963 Chateau Gewirtz, by the way, which I can strongly recommend – and then Mandy mentioned that she was feeling very warm and asked Hazel if we could open a window.

'Hazel shook her head and said: "Darling, I'd rather not let in the cold night air, but if you're feeling hot, why don't you take off your top?"

'This really shocked me because Hazel must have seen that I could hardly keep my eyes off her lovely cousin. However, Mandy didn't seem shocked at all by Hazel's suggestion and a very sexy, eager expression came over her face as she stood up and slowly peeled the top off her shoulders and revealed the fact that she wasn't wearing a slip or a bra! My prick shot up like lightning as I stared as if mesmerised at her proud, uptilted breasts whilst she strolled over to my chair.

'When she saw the effect she was having on me, Mandy giggled and stroked her swollen nipples, making them stand out like small raspberry kisses. "Unhook the catch at the top of my skirt, Nick," she asked sweetly and I gulped wordlessly whilst I did so with trembling hands. Then Mandy kicked off her shoes and tugged down her skirt and panties at the same time. She stepped out of them, sat herself down on the arm of my chair and said: "M'mm, that's much better," as she stretched and ran her hands all over her smooth, silken body.

'I looked over to Hazel and to my surprise, she didn't appear to be in the least bit angry at her cousin's lecherous antics, not even when Mandy turned to me and whispered: "Nick, tell me truthfully, do you think my breasts are too small?"

' "Not at all, they're absolutely perfect for your body," I replied in a rather strained, husky voice. Mandy smiled and said: "That's very nice to hear but my boobs are not so big as Hazel's, are they?

' "Still, it's quality and not quantity that counts, isn't it?" she added whilst she gently pulled my head towards her and guided my nervous lips to her juicy red nipples. By now my cock was threatening to burst out of my trousers as I kissed her erect tittie and slid my hand down to her fluffy pussy hair which was now damp with her pungent love juice. Again I glanced at Hazel and my heart began to pound when I saw her stand up and begin peeling off her clothes as well!

'Whilst I sucked on Mandy's tits and rubbed my finger along her juicy crack, Hazel finished undressing and when she was stark naked, she came over and started stroking my throbbing tool through my trousers. Then Hazel took my free hand and guided it to her moistening mound whilst she massaged her own large breasts right in front of my face.

' "Nick, it's time for you to strip off, so take your hands from our pussies and stand up so we can help you take off your clothes," commanded Hazel and obediently I rose to my feet and the two girls pulled off everything except my Y-fronts. "Let me take them off, Hazel," said Mandy, licking her lips "I'm dying to see if his cock is as thick as you tell me."

'She knelt down and slowly rolled down my pants and she squealed in mock horror as my shaft sprang up like a Jack-in-the-Box in front of her face. "Oooh, you are a big

6

boy, aren't you?" she said softly as she turned round to look at Hazel who was now lying down on the carpet in front of us with her thighs parted and her fingers lazily playing with her pussy.

'Mandy swung round to face Hazel and over her shoulder asked me to sit on the edge of the chair and keep my legs apart. I did as she asked and Mandy reached behind her and grabbed my cock as she heaved herself up on my things and gently lowered herself upon it, working my knob between her luscious love lips deep inside her hot, wet cunt.

'I played with her perky little breasts, flicking and rubbing her hard, elongated nipples whilst she bounced up and down on my pulsating prick, and Mandy and I watched Hazel try to bring herself off by gently fingering her damp quim with one hand and kneading her boobs with the other. "I wanted to fuck Nick from the first moment I met him," Mandy panted heavily, "and he's hung just as you said, thick and meaty, and I'm going to fuck the arse off him till he shoots his spunk inside my tight little cunny."

This naughty talk made Hazel finger herself furiously and whilst the two girls groaned with pleasure, I was trying desperately to prevent Mandy's clinging cunt from milking my quivering cock too quickly, for at the same time I was watching Hazel play with herself on the carpet and I noticed how she was concentrating on looking at my cock gliding in and out of the crimson chink between Mandy's pouting love lips.

' "It isn't fair for us to fuck whilst poor Hazel is left out in the cold," I gasped and at once Mandy understood what I had in mind, for whilst telling me to keep my prick buried inside her, she pulled me down off the chair and we slid down together to join Hazel on the carpet. Then, making sure that my cock was still embedded in her cunny, Mandy leaned forward and slowly lowered her head between Hazel's slender thighs and started to lick out her cousin's pungent pussy.

'This soon drove Hazel completely wild and she began to moan: "Oh yes, yes, don't stop! Now play with my clit and finish me off with your tongue, you wicked girl!"

'Of course this also sent Mandy and me over the top and both girls came several times until I just couldn't hold back any longer and my spunk shot out of my cock like water out of a geyser deep inside Mandy's cunny.

'When we had recovered Mandy said brightly: "Wow! That was a terrific birthday present. Thank you both very much – I've always wanted to suck on a nice pussy whilst I'm being fucked. You really must try it, Hazel, it's a wonderful experience."

'The two girls looked at me and I gave them a glassy smile for my cock was just dangling limply between my thighs. But when Mandy bent down and swirled her wet tongue all along the top of my helmet, my shaft stiffened up almost immediately and a few moments later I was easing Hazel on her back and sliding my shaft into her sopping slit. Mandy moved over to straddle Hazel's face and as she gently lowered her juicy cunney onto her cousin's waiting lips, whilst I was fucking Hazel, I hauled myself up and started to nibble her tender tits. Hazel soon had Mandy coming all over her face and Hazel and I came together a couple of minutes later.'

Nick paused as Chrissie deposited two prawn cocktails on their table and he leaned back in his chair whilst a gleeful smile flashed across his face at the recollection of this steamy encounter. Steve Williams pursed his lips and said with feeling: 'I wish I knew a girl who would invite me to a birthday party like that! So what happened then, Nick? Did you have a quick coffee and then take your leave?'

'Hell, no! I stayed the night and we retired to the bedroom where it was my turn to be on my back and Mandy rested her dripping crack on my lips with her bum resting on my nose, whilst Hazel mounted my cock. I sucked Mandy's delicious pussy while she and Hazel fiddled with each other's boobs. Although I had already spunked twice, it didn't take long for me to come again because Hazel was humping me like mad whilst the taste of Mandy's wet cunt and watching the girls playing with each other were driving me nuts!

'When I'd finished, they rolled off me and began fingering themselves and finished up in a sixty-nine position. Hazel soon had Mandy coming all over her face and she exploded into Mandy's mouth shortly after, and then the three of us just lay on the bed, drenched in each other's juices, and fell fast asleep. Luckily, I woke up early enough in the morning to rouse the girls so that we had time to start again where we had left off, but I only had time to fuck Mandy before we had to get up as none of us could afford to take the day off work. Still, Mandy invited Hazel and me up to Birmingham for an intimate little party next weekend, and I don't mind telling you I can hardly wait to get on the old M1!'

Steve swallowed a mouthful of prawn cocktail and said with a mournful sigh: 'You are a jammy bugger, Nick! And here am I, a poor lad who's been without crumpet for the best part of a month now. Still, as they say, to him that hath it shall be given and he who hath not, tough luck, mate!'

'Now, now, don't feel too sorry for yourself,' chuckled Nick as Oscar placed a decanter of claret in front of him. 'Mandy said she knew her best and very horny friend would want to come to the party so could I bring a nice guy from London to make up the numbers, and straight away I thought I'd give you first refusal. So if you're free,

Steve, be at my pad with a nice bottle of plonk at about six o'clock on Saturday and we'll drive up the motorway in my car. There'll be no hassle about putting the petrol on my expenses because my boss hasn't been looking at them too closely since I managed to persuade the fashion buyer for that big new store in Knightsbridge to stock our autumn range.

'Well, how about it, Steve, can you make Saturday night or do I have to start searching for another cock?'

'I can make it, and thanks very much for thinking of me,' said Steve with genuine gratitude. 'Come hell or high water, I'll be at your flat at six o'clock sharp on Saturday night.'

Nick winked at his friend. 'That's the spirit! We'll have a great time shagging ourselves silly and that's just what I need right now after what Simon Barber, our export director, told me this morning.'

'Why? What's up, Nick? I thought all was well with you at work.'

'Oh it is, and in a way I'm the victim of my own success. It seems that the firm plans to make a big push to export our garments later this year,' Nick grunted unhappily, 'and Mr Barber wants me to spearhead the drive into Europe, so he's going to sign me up for an all expenses paid crash course in commercial French at one of these summer schools next month. I'll be away for four weeks starting at the end of July.'

'Well, what's so terrible about that?' demanded Steve. 'It'll mean some foreign travel and probably more money, too. I can't see why you're not jumping for joy.'

Chrissie came up and whisked away the remains of their starters as Nick shrugged his shoulders and said: 'I should be, I suppose, but I'm not so certain that I'm not being given the old white elephant. You know what that expression refers to, don't you?'

When his friend shook his head Nick gave a short laugh and went on: 'It began in the Far East in the last century. It seems that if the King of Siam was exceptionally pleased with one of his generals, he presented him with a white elephant as a token of esteem – but the gift was two-edged because it cost so much to keep one of these fucking elephants that the guy was forced to spend all he owned to keep the beast in good shape.

'It's a wonderful way to stuff someone when you can't attack them directly because they're too popular. Just like the king didn't want any of his chiefs from getting too powerful, I'm damned sure that's why I've been given this new job. I'm a good salesman but a rotten office politician and I think that the rat fink of a home sales director has put me up for this job because he's worried about his own position. I'm the only guy who stands up to him and he wouldn't shed any tears to see me transferred to the export division.'

Steve took a deep breath and slowly exhaled before he replied carefully: 'I hear what you say, mate, and you don't have to tell me anything about office politics. You can imagine what it's like in a huge organisation like the BBC! But aren't you being a bit negative about all this? After all, it must mean a rise and frankly, I think your firm are being very sensible about trying to get a foothold in Europe. Old De Gaulle might veto our application to join the Common Market but we're bound to go in sooner rather than later and you'll be well-placed to reap the benefits.'

'Okay, okay, Simon Barber has been saying much the same thing to me and I suppose it's true enough, but I hate the idea of going back to school to learn French, especially in August when I'd planned to go to Rimini with a couple of mates,' grumbled Nick as Chrissie reappeared with their steaks.

'You're going to learn French, Nick?' she said with interest. 'That was my best subject at school, my teacher said I would have passed A Level if I had decided to go into the sixth form.'

Nick gave her a roguish grin. 'I can well believe it, lovey, and I'm free any night if you want to give me some private lessons in French. You'll find out that I'm a quick learner.'

Chrissie rolled her eyes upwards. 'Men! You know perfectly well I didn't mean *that* kind of French, Nick Armitage. I was talking about the language.'

'So was I,' said Nick innocently as Chrissie plonked down his steak in front of him. 'And believe me, I could do with a refresher course before I go to this bloody summer school. I just about scraped through my French O Level, but I've forgotten practically everything except *Voulez vous coucher avec moi ce soir?*'

'*Non, merci,*' said Chrissie with a giggle and she turned to Steve and asked: 'Could you really arrange an audition for me with the BBC repertory? I'd be ever so grateful.'

Steve looked hard at the pretty face of the coltish, long-legged girl and said hesitatingly: 'Well, I suppose I could try – you haven't ever broadcast before, have you? Then the best thing to do would be to nip into a studio and make a demo tape. You said you've done some Shakespeare at drama school so choose a soliloquy to recite and I'll record it for you.'

She clapped her hands in glee. 'Oh thank you, Steve, you're a star! I'll finish here at three o'clock and I'm off this evening so is there any chance of doing it today?'

'I don't see why not, I'll have a studio free later this afternoon and my assistant will give us a hand. Come to Broadcasting House at five o'clock and we'll put you through your paces,' said Steve, who could not prevent his prick stirring in his pants as he looked directly into the

Meet the Boys

swell of Chrissie's pert breasts and her eyes shone with delight as she leaned forward and kissed him lightly on the forehead.

'See you at five, Steve,' she said and after she skipped happily away Nick chuckled: 'The wheel of fortune's rolling in your direction, you lucky lad, I'd have a flutter on the three-thirty at Kempton Park, you're bound to pick out the winner.'

Steve flushed and raised his voice in protest. 'Hey, just because I'm going to audition Chrissie this afternoon it doesn't mean that—'

'Oh yes it does!' Nick cut in as he leered across the table and added: 'after the audition you'll take her out for a drink and a bite to eat and then you'll go back to her flat for a nightcap and a little rumpy pumpy – or more likely a great deal of rumpy pumpy, if I'm any judge of the situation. Good luck tonight, Steve, just remember our date in Birmingham on Saturday.'

'I won't forget,' Steve promised. 'And whilst I'd like nothing more than to have it away with Chrissie, I don't think I'm in with much of a chance.'

Nick held out his hand. 'A quid says that you'll have her knickers off tonight,' he said. 'Go on, I'll trust you to tell me if I win or lose.'

'No, either way that wouldn't be fair to Chrissie,' Steve demurred. 'But I might well take your advice and put ten bob on a horse this afternoon. Hilary, my assistant, gets some marvellous tips from a trainer who took a shine to her when we were doing a documentary about the Derby last year. Of course, they don't all come up trumps but we've had more winners than losers and Hilary, who puts a pound on all the horses, says she's well in profit. For what it's worth, this guy told us to put a fiver each way on Bayswater Boy in the four o'clock at Sandown today, but don't blame me if the

13

horse is still running tomorrow morning!'

'Must be an outsider,' mused Nick as he pulled out a pen and scribbled the name on the back of the menu card which he slipped into his pocket. 'I'm obliged to you, Steve, it's always worth having a bob or two on a nag when you know the jockey's really trying. I'll pop into the betting shop over the road on our way out.'

The two friends enjoyed the rest of their lunch and when they rose from the table, Steve felt a warm glow of anticipation run through his body as Chrissie helped him on with his coat and blew him a kiss as she murmured throatily: 'See you at five, and thanks again for all the trouble you're taking for me.'

Outside the club, Nick waved goodbye and disappeared into the betting shop where he placed a pound each way on Bayswater Boy whose starting price hovered around the twenty-five to one mark. Steve hurried back to Broadcasting House where he planned to spend the rest of the afternoon editing out the fluffs made by the presenter during an interview with a famous author which was due to be broadcast on an arts programme over the coming weekend.

But when Steve arrived back at his office, there was a note on his desk from Hilary, his production assistant, telling him that the senior administrator for radio drama wanted to see him as soon as he came back from lunch. He looked at his watch and noted with relief that it was only twenty past two as he picked up the internal telephone and dialled his boss's number.

'Hello, Mr Harvill, Steve Williams here, I understand that you wanted to see me. What? Yes, sure, I'll come up right away,' he said, putting down the receiver, wondering what on earth the administrator could want with him.

However, he soon found out that there was nothing to

fear, for Edward Harvill was obviously in a good mood as he waved at Steve to take a chair. After a few pleasantries, his boss leaned over his desk and said: 'Steve, I'll come straight to the point. I had a memo from the Governor's Office the other day about how we need to promote ourselves more to the general public. There's still an important audience for radio drama but it's aging and the powers that be want us to attract a new group of younger listeners. I don't know whether it's possible to wean teenagers away from television but we must be seen to have made a stab at it.

'Anyhow, Stephen, the point is that a Doctor Edwin Radleigh, the principal of Falmington on Sea College of Further Education, has asked us if we could provide a guest lecturer for a course they want to run in the summer school curriculum on Writing Radio Drama In The Sixties and I thought you would be the ideal chap for the job.

'The course lasts throughout August and as I understand you're not taking your holiday till September, taking time out for four weeks beforehand would give you six full weeks away from the office to recharge the old batteries. All your living expenses will be paid for by the College and Dr Radleigh says that the lecturer will be put up in a four star hotel near the college. Now I can't order you to give these lectures, but I need hardly say that if you oblige me by spending August down at Falmington, I certainly won't forget you when next year's salary review comes up in November.'

If he had but known, Mr Harvill had little need to hold out the bait of extra money, for the idea of lecturing to a group of young students quite appealed to Steve who was very much a radio man and – except for sport and an occasional documentary – far preferred the older medium to television.

15

'I'll be happy to go, sir,' said Steve, taking Dr Radleigh's letter which Mr Harvill was offering to him. 'Shall I answer Dr Radleigh directly or will you reply?'

'Oh, I'll reply and tell the good doctor to contact you directly with all the details,' said his boss with evident satisfaction. 'You were my first choice for this important job, Stephen, and I'm sure that you'll be a credit to the BBC.'

Mr Harvill escorted Steve to the door and patted him on the shoulder. 'Good luck, my boy, I'll leave everything in your hands. Keep me informed on what happens – who knows, if this turns out to be a success, we might even run some lectures ourselves before an invited audience of listeners on the future of radio which we could then broadcast on the Home Service.'

Back in his office, a thought suddenly struck Steve and he picked up his telephone and dialled Nick Armitage's work number. Although Falmington was only a small seaside resort about ten miles outside Brighton, the town's college was noted for the excellence of its summer courses. Was it possible that Nick was also going to Falmington in August?

'Blair and Lessner? Nick Armitage, please,' he said to the telephonist and he only had to wait for a few seconds before his friend was on the line. 'Nick, hi there, it's Steve. You won't credit it, but I'm also going to summer school in August. I've been asked to give a series of lectures on radio drama and I was wondering whether by happy coincidence we might find ourselves at the same college.'

'Hold on, I'll check the file,' said Nick and then a few moments later he came back and said: 'I'm going to some godforsaken little place near Brighton called Falmington On Sea. That's where you're going? Great news, man! At least we'll be able to have some fun together after work.

Thanks for calling, Steve, see you on Saturday if not before.'

Steve replaced the receiver and punched the air in triumph. The day really was going well and if Lady Luck continued to shine on him he would later enjoy a fabulous evening with Chrissie. For the next hour he tackled some outstanding paperwork and then just before five o'clock he called the Sports Desk to check how Bayswater Boy had fared at Sandown.

'Put the phone down, I can tell you that he romped home at sixteen to one. The odds would have been longer but there was a last-minute rush of money on him at the course, no doubt from colleagues of our tipster buddy,' said Hilary, his attractive production assistant, who had heard him ask about Bayswater Boy's fate as she had walked into the office. 'Good news all round, wouldn't you say?'

'Good news for my friend Nick Armitage who followed your tip, but bad news for me as I didn't bother to have a bet,' said Steve sadly.

'Yes you did,' beamed Hilary as she fished out a betting slip from her handbag. 'Honestly, Steve, you *are* getting absentminded. Don't you remember giving me a pound note in the BBC Club to put ten bob each way for you? I also put ten bob each way so we'll both collect a tenner. You don't mind if I pop out for five minutes and draw our ill-gotten gains, do you? Audrey Hendon from Documentaries is getting married this weekend and I'm going to her hen party tonight at The Garment District, so the cash will come in very handy.'

'The Garment District? That's not the sort of place I'd have a hen party,' remarked Steve who was naturally delighted at being reminded that he had backed Bayswater Boy after all. 'A stag night, maybe, but girls wouldn't want to see one of those raunchy cabarets.'

17

'Perhaps not, but Audrey's husband-to-be is the club's solicitor and our little shindig will be in one of the private suites, and I wouldn't be surprised if we won't have some special entertainment laid on for us,' replied Hilary as the telephone rang and she answered in a brisk voice: 'Steven Williams' office, can I help you?'

She turned to Steve and said: 'There's a girl named Chrissie Brownlow in reception to see you. Is this business or pleasure?'

With luck it could be both, said Steve to himself as he cleared his throat and told Hilary how Nick Armitage had asked him to give this struggling young actress a chance to audition for the BBC repertory company. Then he added: 'Why don't you go and collect our loot? And whilst you're downstairs you can ask one of the commissionaires to bring Chrissie up to the office.'

'Okay, Steve,' agreed Hilary, picking up her handbag. 'I'll be as quick as possible. Now are you sure you can handle a struggling young actress all by yourself? I hope you'll know what to do if she starts tearing your clothes off when you tell her that she has an explosive latent talent deep within her inner being!'

'Now, now, don't be naughty, you know perfectly well that particular line belongs to Brian Stanstead,' replied Steve, mentioning the name of his colleague who was noted for bedding more aspiring actresses than any previous producer in the department. He ruffled through his drawer to find a booking form for the small studio across the corridor and went on: 'When you come back, come into the studio and give me your opinion about her.'

A few minutes later, a doorman ushered Chrissie into the office. Steve stood up and caught his breath at the sight of the gorgeous, sweet-faced girl with her mane of tousled tawny hair which ran over her slender shoulders. She reminded him of his first serious girlfriend who also wore her hair long, but Toni's snub nose had been dusted with tiny freckles whilst Chrissie's nose was equally small but slightly tip-tilted with pretty little nostrils, and underneath were wide, generous red lips. She was wearing a figure-hugging green minidress which accentuated the thrust of her breasts whilst showing off her ravishingly slim figure and long legs and Steve's voice shook slightly as he gulped: 'Hello again, Chrissie, take a seat. I'll just fix up things with the studio manager so when my assistant comes back we can begin. She won't be long, but can I get you a tea or coffee whilst we wait for her?'

'No thanks, Steve, I'll just get my material ready,' she said as she sat down and crossed her legs, her skirt riding high up to reveal the upper part of her smooth thigh.

He could scarcely take his eyes off Chrissie as he made the short telephone call to book the studio. 'What would you like to do for me?' he asked, suppressing an inward laugh as the thought flashed across his mind that he would love to frame the answer to that question.

'I decided to start with a couple of pieces from the Scottish play,' she answered, holding to the old theatrical tradition of it being unlucky to mention Shakespeare's *Macbeth* by name. 'The first from Act One when Lady M. has to psyche herself up to persuade her husband to murder the king.'

Steve nodded and said: 'Oh, you mean the lines which begin: "*Come, you spirits that tend on mortal thoughts, unsex me here*".' He gave a short, nervous laugh and went on: 'Listen, Chrissie, I have to admit that if you can make me think of you unsexed, you'll waltz into the BBC rep!'

Two delicious dimples appeared on her cheeks as she smiled and said: 'Well thank you, kind sir. And let me say how impressed I am about your knowledge of the play. It was my favourite out of all the works of Shakespeare we pored through at drama school.'

'Yes, I also enjoyed Mac–, oops, I nearly blew it, when we studied the play at school,' said Steve, clicking his fingers in irritation as he realised that he nearly uttered the dreaded word! 'I suppose your second piece will be the mad scene? "*Out damned spot! Out I say!*" – I'll take the part of The Doctor and Hilary can play The Gentle-woman. Now what else would you like to read? Something light, perhaps, to make a nice contrast with the heavy stuff?'

'I've a couple of poems and a short comic monologue,' she replied as Steve walked to the door and said: 'I'll just book the studio – back in a minute, love.'

Before the audition, Steve would have readily admitted that he had not entertained high hopes of her abilities, but he was pleasantly surprised to discover that Chrissie possessed a genuine talent and even Hilary (who had guessed that her boss had been smitten by this sexy, tawny-haired beauty) had been impressed by Chrissie's performance.

The stunning girl made full use of her sensual, slightly sibilant voice and after Steve had played back the tape it was with complete sincerity he told Chrissie that in his opinion, she had an excellent chance of being asked to join the prestigious BBC company of actors who were favoured not only by the radio drama team, but also by casting directors over at the BBC-TV Centre in Shepherds Bush.

'I'll send the tape through to Beth Macdougall first thing in the morning with a note recommending that you should be considered for the rep and in the meantime, how would you like to play Maria in *Twelfth Night* which we're recording for the Home Service in six weeks time? Elizabeth Thomson has asked to back out as Dickie Attenborough wants her for his new film and I must find a replacement in the next few days. The money won't be wonderful but we've been lucky enough to get together a great cast. We'll have Patrick Janson-Smith as Malvolio, Sally Randall as Olivia and Nicholas Webb as Sir Toby Belch. Quite an all-star line up so I'm sure the production will be noticed by the critics.'

'Oh, that would be marvellous,' gasped Chrissie, wringing her hands together in surprised delight. 'But Steve, do you honestly think I'm up to it? Just the thought of working with people like Sally Randall and Nicholas Webb is already giving me butterflies in my tummy!'

'Of course you are! If I didn't think so, I wouldn't have offered you the part. I want to keep my job, you know!'

Hilary patted her on the shoulder and said firmly: 'You'll be fine, Chrissie, there's no need to be nervous. I've worked with Sally Randall before and she's a really nice person who never throws about any of that I-am-a-star-so-I-must-be-treated-like-royalty bullshit. And don't worry about the men, you'll have them eating out of your hand. Which reminds me, I must dash, I've a party to go to. Nice meeting you, Chrissie, we'll meet again soon at the first rehearsal. Cheerio, Steve, see you tomorrow.'

'Bye, Hilary, thanks again,' he replied and smiled as he looked at Chrissie whose face was aglow with happiness. 'Now, who's your agent? I'll write and confirm the offer to him. And then I hope you'll join me in a celebration drink round the corner at the BBC Club.'

'I'm with Noel Amos at Erica Major Management and yes, I'd love a drink, that would be super. God, I just can't believe this is happening to me. Give me a pinch, Steve, so I'll know I'm not just in the middle of a lovely dream.'

He reached out and grasped her hand, gently stroking her long, delicate fingers. 'There, will that convince you?' he grinned as she took his hand between hers and gave it a gentle squeeze. 'I won't forget your kindness,' she promised and for a moment their eyes locked together before

Steve gave a little cough and said: 'Right, I'll note down your agent's name and then before we go I must make a quick call to my flat-mate to see if I've had any 'phone calls.'

'Ah ha, who's the lucky girl?' Chrissie twinkled as he picked up the telephone and dialled the number.

'Chance would be a fine thing,' he replied promptly. 'His name's Mark Adams and he's the night news editor of the *Daily Graphic*. I should catch him just before he goes to work. My dad slipped off a stepladder last week and hurt his back so I want to know if my mum's called to let me know if he's feeling any better.'

Happily, Steve caught Mark before he left the flat for Fleet Street and his flat-mate passed on the good news that Steve's mother had indeed telephoned to tell him that his father was now back to full fitness and was planning to return to work in the morning.

Everything's coming up roses, thought Steve, as he escorted Chrissie to the lifts and all continued to go well for him in the BBC Club where they enjoyed a quiet drink and Chrissie was able to stare with interest at several well-known BBC personalities who drifted into the bar. She nearly choked with excitement when Steve introduced her to Roger Tagholm, the scriptwriter of *Fred's*, one of the most popular situation comedies on television, and after he had left them she whispered to Steve: 'Isn't he nice? And he must be so clever to write such a funny show week after week. When did you meet him?'

'A couple of months ago I produced a kind of *Desert Island Discs* programme which will go out during the summer for a short run. It's called *Classical Choice* and in each programme a celebrity not associated with the arts told listeners all about their favourite piece of music which we then played. We had a good mixed bag of people like a Cabinet Minister, a couple of footballers and a chat-show host – and I think that Roger was the very first guest.'

'What did he choose?' asked Chrissie. 'Something well-known by Mozart or Beethoven, I would guess.'

'You'd be wrong,' he replied. 'It appears that he's very much into Eastern sounds and we had to play a pretty weird example of twentieth century Indian music. It was so way-out that I'm still wondering whether he played a practical joke on us!'

'I quite like Indian music – and I love Indian food,' remarked Chrissie and Steve exclaimed: 'Well, so do I! Have you been to the Akash in Margaret Street? It's really superb. Look, why don't we have a bite of supper there? I'm sure you'll like it.'

Chrissie hesitated for a minute but he went on: 'Oh, do come. Hey, there are no strings attached. You'll have your audition and you'll be in *Twelfth Night*, that's all fixed. I would love to take you out for a meal, but you don't have to accept because you feel you owe me anything.'

Her delicious dimples appeared again as she smiled and said: 'I *do* owe you but I'd love to have dinner with you because I like you as a person and not just because you're doing so much for me.'

She squeezed his hand and Steve could not resist kissing her lightly on the cheek before he finished his glass of white wine which he set down on the table in front of them.

They both thoroughly enjoyed the excellent food at the Akash and Chrissie did not demur when Steve suggested that they have coffee at his flat. He thrilled to the feel of her soft body as she snuggled against him in the taxi as they sped northwards through Regent's Park to his flat in St John's Wood.

'I'm afraid it will only be instant,' he said apologetically as he put his arm around her. 'That's what they all say,' she whispered and Steve gave a throaty chuckle as he pulled her closer to him.

Inside his flat, Chrissie looked round approvingly. 'What a nice pad! And everything's so nice and tidy! You'd never guess two guys were living here,' she remarked as Steve took her coat.

'We have a very nice lady who comes twice a week to clean up after us,' he explained. 'Mrs Sims was here this afternoon so you're seeing us at our best. Now, what can I offer you whilst I put on the kettle? We're very well stocked because whilst I worked on a pop music programme last month, all the song pluggers came into the office with crates of booze when they found out it was my birthday. So what will Madame have from the bar – a cognac, cointreau, drambuie, kummel?'

Five minutes later they were sitting together on the settee sipping cognac with their coffee listening to the smooth voice of Frank Sinatra singing *Autumn Leaves*. 'Early autumn's my favourite time of year,' murmured Steve and he went on: '*Season of mists and mellow fruitfulness, close bosom-friend of the maturing sun.*'

Chrissie put her finger to his lips and she continued: '*Conspiring with him how to load and bless, with fruit the vines that round the thatch-eves run;*' She lifted her face to him and Steve lowered his lips onto hers, kissing her head as they held each other tightly in an urgent embrace.

When Chrissie's tongue began flashing from side to side inside his mouth, Steve's cock uncurled into a rock hard rod which formed a mountainous bulge in his lap and his hand trembled as he cupped one of her jutting breasts.

'Wait a minute,' she whispered and Steve withdrew his hand immediately and said: 'Oh, I'm sorry, I was so carried away by—'

The gorgeous girl giggled softly and said: 'No, I liked it,

you silly boy. I don't want to crease my dress, that's all.'
And with that she broke away from him and stood up and
walked across the room, swinging her hips to the lazy beat
of the music as she unzipped her dress and let it slip to the
floor. She wore no slip and Steve watched in awe as her
proud, thrusting breasts jiggled sensuously in the scanty
shells of her bra before she reached round and unclipped
it, pulling off the garment from the front and throwing it
onto a chair. Then she smoothed her hands over her
pointy strawberry nipples and walked slowly towards him
clad only in a pair of tiny white bikini panties which barely
covered her pubic mound, moulding the swell of her pussy
lips which made Steve quiver with desire as she
approached him.

Chrissie now stood directly in front of him with her
hands on his shoulders and he ran his fingers slowly across
the thin silky material of her panties. She opened her legs
a little wider and Steve cupped his hand over her pussy
and then slipped his fingers underneath her panties to feel
her wetness.

'Well now, does Sir want to make a purchase or shall I
wrap the goods up again?' asked Chrissie with a mocking
smile upon her pretty face.

'Oh no, don't do that! I've a far better idea, let's put out
everything on display,' Steve replied huskily as he rolled
her panties over her hips down to her ankles. He buried
his face in the thick forest of curly hair which adorned
Chrissie's cunt and closing his eyes, he inhaled deeply the
exquisite musky perfume emanating from the sexually
aroused girl's groin. Raising his head he extended his
tongue and ran it with warm, wet lasciviousness along the
full length of her cunny lips, from front to back, pausing
now and then to savour more fully the intoxicating cuntal
aroma.

He heard a low crooning noise coming from Chrissie's

throat which sent a thrilling current of anticipation shuddering through him. He had always loved the noises girls make when they get excited and then he himself moaned with delight when he felt her hand reach down and unzip his fly. His cock sprang out of his trousers and Chrissie's fingers circled his shaft and slid rhythmically up and down its length.

Steve kept his lips pressed to her pussy as he tore off his clothes and only when he too was naked, he lifted his face from her curly thatch and hauling himself up to his feet, led her by the hand into his bedroom. They threw themselves down upon the bed, locking themselves into a passionate embrace and looked steadily into her beautiful brown eyes and murmured: 'Chrissie, I must ask you, are you—'

She answered him before he could complete the question. 'Yes, yes, I'm on the pill and I want you to shoot your sticky spunk inside me,' she panted wildly. 'Empty your balls in my honeypot, Steve, I want your creamy jism to drench my cunt.'

He mounted her and she grasped his pulsing prick and guided his knob between her rubbery love lips. Her cunney was deliciously lubricated and after after two or three strokes his cock was coated with her pussy juices. Chrissie came almost immediately, her thighs clasping him in a vice as the force of her orgasm spread out through every fibre of her body.

He continued to pump in and out of her luscious love channel whilst her fingernails dug into his back, and the combined perspiration of their lust cemented their public hairs together as their bodies thrashed back and forth with Chrissie raising her hips to meet Steve's powerful thrusts.

Steve grunted with ecstasy as his shaft slid along the walls of her love channel. Chrissie's frame vibrated like a taut wire as he kept up his steady thrusting, and to her delight he varied the length of his strokes as he shifted his position from time to time. She squealed with delight as he took his weight upon his hands and watched his rigid rod slide in and out between her yielding cunny lips.

Then she crossed her legs over his back and began moving her tongue inside his mouth faster and faster as her cunt squeezed his pulsating prick so superbly that his climax came upon him almost at once and with a hoarse cry he shot a torrent of hot, glutinous jism inside her, filling her juice box and splashing against the soft folds of her pussy.

They lay kissing and cuddling before Steve withdrew his deflated shaft and fell back exhausted onto his pillow. As he had told Nick Armitage at lunchtime, it had been the best part of a month since he had broken up with his last girlfriend, a secretary in the drama department who had decided to end the relationship and take up a job with Granada TV in Manchester, and no other girl had yet taken her place in his lonely bed.

Yet though the muscles in his thighs and arms were throbbing from the pleasant but strenuous exercise he had just undertaken, there were still vivid images of Chrissie's proud, jutting breasts and of her pouting pussy lips peeking through the fringe of silky brown curls racing through Steve's brain as he lay with his eyes closed and his chest heaving up and down as he fought to regain his composure.

His cock drooped at half-mast over his thigh but then he felt Chrissie's cool hands smooth themselves along his body. Steve opened his eyes to see her mane of tawny hair slide across his chest as Chrissie kissed his nipples, and then she moved her head downwards towards his groin where his cock was now uncoiling upwards and she stopped there to swirl the tip of her tongue over his uncapped helmet.

'A-a-a-g-h!' he moaned as Chrissie now moved her head further downwards to lick the loose pink skin of his scrotum, causing his balls to contract and tighten. Then opening wide her generous lips, she took his ballsack fully into her mouth, encircling it wetly with her tongue and lightly squeezing with extreme care, making Steve cry out in delight from the sheer rapture of the sensation which was causing his heart to hammer wildly in his heaving chest.

Chrissie now concentrated on his turgid, throbbing boner, running her tongue along its length from base to knob before popping it into her mouth and slowly lowering her head to engulf it more fully. Breathing deeply through her nose with her nostrils flared, she almost swooned at the erotic, earthy scent of the remains of Steve's spunk from his previous spend as she raised and lowered her head with increasing rapidity, exerting ever more pressure with her lips which further magnified Steve's sensual pleasure.

Almost involuntarily he jabbed his cock upwards, trying to jam his tool as far down her throat as possible and she continued to gobble greedily on his fleshy pole as she knelt across him, the soft white spheres of her bottom just inches away from his face. Steve pulled them slightly apart to see her wrinkled little bum-hole and, at the centre of his vision, the dusky pink oyster folds of her exquisite cunt which beckoned his lips with a compellingly succulent intensity.

He licked and lapped her juicy pussy and then he sank a finger between her bum cheeks which took Chrissie over the top. She came in great wheezing shudders, bouncing up and down on his face and her orgasm went on and on, but she never released her hold on his bursting cock which now gushed out jism down her throat like water from a hose.

Afterwards they lay in a sticky heap for some time until Chrissie squirmed around to plant a firm, wet kiss on his lips. Steve held her tight and then pulling the eiderdown over them, they fell fast asleep.

However, at about the same time, in Nick Armitage's luxuriously fitted bedroom in a small, purpose-built block of luxury apartments just off the King's Road, a young couple were on the verge of waking up from their slumbers. Marcella, the blonde dolly-bird who was the receptionist at Gottlieb Textiles where Nick worked, stirred as she felt his elbow dig into her ribs. She turned round and saw Nick moving restlessly from side to side and she wondered if he was having a bad dream and whether it would be best to rouse him. But she was spared having to make the decision for a few seconds later Nick opened his eyes and said: 'Ooof! What a horrible dream! Hey, why are you awake, Marcie? Did I disturb you?'

'I'm afraid you did, you were tossing around like crazy,' she answered, looking at him with a frown of concern forming across her forehead. 'Nick, is there something on your mind? To be honest you weren't your usual happy self this evening. Didn't you enjoy the picture?'

'Very much,' said Nick although he had been disappointed that *Elvira Madigan*, a Swedish film that had won such high praise from the critics had no explicit love scenes and was simply a beautifully photographed though sad romantic idyll about a married army officer and a dancer who run off and finally commit suicide rather than part.

'And I enjoyed you even more, Marcella Whitfield!' he added as he leaned across and kissed her cheek. 'I'm sorry I woke you, I usually sleep like a log but just now there's something on my mind which is worrying me.'

The attractive girl shifted herself up and placed a comforting hand on his shoulder. 'What's the matter,

Nick? Is it something at work? If it is, I bet I can guess what your problem is – you don't want to take up that place at the summer school which Simon Barber has arranged for you.'

Nick looked at her in astonishment. 'Good God, how did you know about it?' he blurted out. 'Besides Simon and myself, I thought that only Mr Gottlieb knew about the idea. Still, it's hardly a state secret and I should have known that the news would travel through the office grapevine.'

Marcella smiled her agreement but persevered and said: 'You'd be surprised what I hear in the reception area, Nick. Some of the stupid sods who work with you either forget I'm sitting at the desk or think I'm just a dumb blonde who won't understand what they're talking about. I'm right, though, aren't I? For some reason, you're worried about going to that summer school.'

'You're quite right,' he admitted as he snuggled himself down, placing his head between Marcella's large breasts, and he told her as he had explained to Steven Williams earlier in the day the reasons for his concern.

Marcella was as surprised as Steve had been that Nick was not jumping at the chance to learn another language. 'It's another string to your bow, you silly boy,' she said decisively. 'And even if there are people after your job in the firm, with some export experience under your belt you can please yourself whether or not you want to stay where you are, because there'll be lots of other companies keen to offer you a job and you can tell Alan Gottlieb to fuck himself.'

He gave a wry smile and said: 'I don't want to do that, it's not Alan who is giving me any hassle, he's a good guy. I'd like to stay with him as I think he's going to build the company up into something big. Look how the firm's grown since he took over from his uncle eighteen months ago.'

'I'm glad to hear you say that because I like Alan too. He took me out to the Caprice for my birthday, you know, and

I've only been with the company for about eight months,' remarked Marcella, sliding her hand downwards to grasp Nick's flaccid penis. 'Oo-er, what's happened to your little friend, Mr Armitage, doesn't he like me any more?'

'Of course he does,' Nick replied sleepily. 'I'm just tired, that's all. Tell you what, Marcie, tell me all about your evening with Alan Gottlieb, that's bound to turn me on. Is it true he's hung like a donkey?'

Marcella let out an exasperated sigh. 'You men, you're obsessed about the size of your dicks! How many times do you have to be told that it isn't the size of the ship that counts but the motion of the ocean! Mind you, it's true enough that Alan Gottlieb does have an enormous cock, it must be at least ten inches long, and I was to find out that he certainly knows how to use it.'

'Did he take you up to the company flat in St John's Wood after dinner?' asked Nick as he nuzzled his lips against her left nipple. 'Simon Barber told me that's where he takes his special friends.'

She gave a brief nod and went on: 'Yes, if you must know. We had a wonderful dinner at the Caprice and then Alan drove me back to the flat where I made some coffee and we sat together on the sofa talking about football, would you believe! Alan's an Arsenal fan like me and he promised to get me a ticket for the match against Manchester United next month.'

'He didn't try to kiss you?' wondered Nick and Marcella laid a reproving hand on his head. 'No, he was the perfect gentleman. Too perfect in a way because by now I was feeling quite randy and more than ready for a little nookie, especially because it's always the men who don't come on so heavy which attract me more.

'And before you say it, you're the exception to the rule!' she added playfully, ruffling his hair before she continued: 'All right, I'll carry on if listening to me gives you a hard-on. Well, he poured us out a beautifully smooth vintage brandy to drink with our coffee and then he suddenly said: 'Marcella, would you like to see a book of erotic photographs from New York which I bought the other day from a little shop I know in the Charing Cross Road? You won't be shocked, will you?'

'No, of course not,' I said and he leaned over and pulled a large leather-bound book off the side table next to the sofa. He opened it up and we leafed through the pages and honest to God, Nick, I've never seen such rude photographs before! All the boys had gigantic stiffies and the girls were shown rubbing, sucking and fucking these big purple pricks. What really turned me on, though, was a set of pictures with one young black stud who was lying naked on his back with six girls around him. Two were kneeling beside him with his fingers tickling their cunnies whilst he diddled two more girls with his toes. Another girl crouched over him with her head facing the headboard and whilst he licked out her cunt, she pushed out her bum towards the sixth girl, who was spitted on the tip of his huge cock.

'I looked at this picture for about a minute and I felt my pussy getting damp as at last Alan's arm slid behind my back and I moved closer to him, allowing my thigh to nestle against his, and I placed his hand on my knee to make sure he fully understood the message.

'Then he kissed me, at first ever so lightly on my cheek and then a second time more firmly on my lips and I fell into this second kiss as if I were lying down in a nice warm bubble bath. His lips were parted and moist and our tongues slid effortlessly into each other's mouths as his hands roamed across my breasts where my nipples were poking their way through my silk blouse and sheer bra. I could see a massive bulge in his lap through his trousers and I started to tingle all over as I imagined what that colossal cock would feel like planted firmly inside my pussy.

'Our mouths stayed glued together as Alan now let his hand ride up my thigh until his fingers ran over my stocking-top. He began to twang the elastic of my suspenders as he started to undo them and I parted my legs so he could finish the job. For the next few minutes we just sat kissing and caressing each other as he slowly undressed me until all I had on was a pair of white cotton knickers.

'I was now so impatient to be fucked that I kisse⌐ his earlobe and breathed softly: "Come on, Alan, I know you brought me here to seduce me, didn't you? Well, go on, I'm ready, willing and able!"

'A sensual smile spread across his face whilst I gave him this green light, and he cupped my bare breast in his hand whilst we dissolved into another passionate French kiss. Then Alan bent his head down and began circling my left tittie with his tongue before taking it inside his mouth. I shuddered all over in absolute ecstasy for it was like he was sucking a nerve-ending which extended all the way down to my pussy, and all I could think of was how much I wanted to fuck him.

'He unbuckled his belt and he raised his bum off the sofa whilst I helped him pull off his trousers and pants and release the rock-hard cock which sprung up and saluted me as I wrapped my hand round the barrel of his thick tool. Then he tore off his shirt and tie and with trembling hands he tugged down my knickers. My nipples were erect and my cunt was now aching for his throbbing fat shaft as I lay back on the sofa and spread my legs. He clambered on top of me and inched his lips down towards my bush. He moved his mouth to my inner thighs and I let out a fierce moan as he made me come with his tongue and fingers.

' "Let's turn you over," said Alan as he flipped me over onto my front and slid a cushion underneath my tummy, wetting his fingers with the love liquid which was running down my thigh. "What a sticky little honeypot you have," he whispered in my ear and just the flow of his breath sent a crackle of a miniature spend flying through my body. At last he slithered his colossal cock between the jiggling cheeks of my backside and I pushed my bum out, wanting him in as deep as he could go. His balls slapped against my bottom as he slewed his shaft in and out of my juicy cunt and I reared and bucked like a lunatic when he pressed his thumb into my arse-hole.

'We teetered on the brink and he came first, pistoning his thick prick in and out of my hungry hole. He started to spunk on an out-stroke, creaming my cunny in a flood of frothy goo, and I quivered all over as a marvellous orgasm shook me from head to toe whilst Alan emptied his balls and collapsed on top of me.'

Marcella had correctly guessed that her carnal confession had stiffened Nick Armitage's cock, and she purred with satisfaction when she reached down and stroked his hard, throbbing boner which was pressing against her leg.

'M'mm, this nice big stiffie seems ready for action,' she commented and Nick grunted his agreement as he buried his face in her luscious breasts whilst at the same time letting his fingers make gentle encircling strokes around her clitty, slow and then faster and faster.

Then he suddenly stopped and sat up, poised above her body, and Marcella closed her eyes in anticipation as his palpitating prick traced a path down her stomach into her thick thatch of blonde hair. Nick adored Marcella's silky pubic bush and could never fathom out why one or two of his friends were turned on by getting their girlfriends to trim their minges. 'How could any guy want to scratch his chin on stubble instead of licking through a sweet forest in full bloom – especially when it adorns a sensuous pouting cunt such as Marcella's?' he would ask with genuine surprise.

But now all that was on Nick's mind was the soft, quivering body of the gorgeous girl underneath him and with a swift, strong stroke he entered her. The slick helmet of his cock slowly caressed her clitty, over and over, then down, then up until Marcella's cunt was so wet that the sheet was slippery between her moving bum cheeks.

He lunged forward and pistoned his prick deep inside her and then began fucking her in a firm, regular rhythm whilst Marcella tensed her trembling legs and raised her buttocks to meet his fierce thrusts, panting with passion until her sweat-sheened breasts jiggled sensuously as she writhed from side to side, and then she uttered a shrill cry of joy as her pussy muscles contracted in a rapid, shivering motion against Nick's cock before they relaxed in the fiery glow of a magnificent climax.

This magical, rippling pressure around his shaft immediately sent Nick over the top and now it was his turn to cry out with pleasure as his sticky spunk spilled out in pulsing jets into the slippery depths of Marcella's soaking love channel.

Nick swung himself off her and lay beside his happy bed-mate, his head resting on his pillow whilst he recovered from his exertions. But Marcella's appetite was not yet sated and a deep chuckle escaped from his throat as he felt her hands fondling his semi-erect shaft, capping and uncapping his gleaming helmet as she slicked her fist up and down his fast-stiffening joystick.

Then Marcella scrambled to her knees and took his tackle in both hands, one dipping to fondle the tightening balls at the base, the other halfway up the shaft. Bending the stem to her mouth, she ran her tongue up to the rim and over the glistening scarlet knob and Nick growled with delight as he watched her lips close over the dome of his twitching tool which swayed slightly as Marcella worked her tongue slowly up and down the length of his erection. She sucked on the sensitive underside of his prick, slurping her way down the velvet-skinned root, skilfully manoeuvring her deliciously wet mouth until she had taken almost all of his shaft between her lips.

He clamped his hands on her head as Marcella circled the base of his boner with her hand and began to bob her head up and down as she gobbled his cock with evident gusto. Nick moaned as she let his tadger fall from her mouth, but she slid her fist up and down his veiny shaft whilst she nibbled on the wrinkled pink skin of his ballsack which sent him into fresh paroxysms of pleasure.

However when he began to groan: 'I'm coming, I'm coming,' Marcella filled her mouth with saliva and again palated his prick as Nick moved his hips up and down to jerk his prick between her lips for a few seconds before he let out a loud sigh and a hot gush of jism cascaded out of his cock which she gulped down without hesitation, smacking her lips as she milked his member dry until she opened her lips and his shaft shrank down to dangle flaccidly over his balls.

'That was tasty, very tasty,' she murmured sleepily as she snuggled into the crook of Nick's shoulder and, in next to no time, the exhausted lovers fell fast asleep in each other's arms.

Some six miles away in St John's Wood, Steven Williams and Chrissie Brownlow were also entwined deep in slumber and neither of the couples woke up to see the first rays of bright spring sunshine light up the quiet London streets.

However, by seven o'clock in a small, one-bedroomed flat only three minutes walk away from Steve's more salubrious apartment, one of the two tousle-haired girls who had been sleeping together in a double bed yawned and opened her eyes. Then she glanced at the bedside clock and groaned . . .

# CHAPTER TWO

## *And Now The Girls . . .*

Denise Cochran stretched out her arms and scowled as she looked for a second time at the clock. Hell's bells, there was no mistaking the time, it was almost five past seven and if she wanted to enjoy even a quick soak in the bath, she would have to get up in ten minutes at the latest. Next to her, Jenny Forsyth was still sleeping, but she worked nearby and did not have to rise until eight o'clock.

This could be an important day for Denise and it was essential that at nine-fifteen sharp she was sitting at her desk opening her mail in the plush Mayfair offices of Chelmsford and Parrish, a small but old-established publishing house. In under eighteen months she had risen from the secretarial ranks to become a junior editor where one of her main tasks was to read through the 'slush pile', the unsolicited manuscripts from hopeful scribes which rained in remorselessly week after week into the postroom.

As at all general publishers, the editors at Chelmsford and Parrish (or C and P, as they were known in the trade) only commissioned books from established authors or from showbiz and sporting personalities who were then helped to produce their memoirs by a skilful set of ghost-writers. The rest of the company's list of new titles came from literary agents who represented those writers who the agencies believed would make the grade and get published – for only then would they get anything from their fifteen per cent share of the author's earnings.

Although a swift glance was often enough for Denise to reach for a paperclip and a rejection slip, this never appeared to dissuade would-be writers from flooding C and P with a deluge of paper for Denise to wade through. But as her boss, George Radlett, had said to her when he offered her the chance to move up from typing his correspondence, once in a while a nugget appears amongst the dross.

'That's why we have to read through all this stuff,' he had told her earnestly. 'The diamond you're looking for is very probably unpolished, but the person who can fish out a bestseller from the slush pile becomes as fêted in the trade as the actual author. Remember *Twilight In Sevenoaks* by Roger Palmer? That came from the slush pile. I grant you we had to reshape and edit it quite a bit but it was a great seller for us, and even bigger of course for Penguin who'll republish when the film comes out next year. And you know what happened to Belinda Nayland, the girl who discovered the the original manuscript? I offered a big rise and a chance to be a commissioning editor but Bob Cripps of Shackleton's offered her two hundred and fifty pounds a year more than I could go and that's why you're now being offered her job!'

At first the work had been exciting although she soon tired of reading through lots of dreary, dog-eared manuscripts, and it had been at least eight weeks since she had found anything worth taking to George Radlett for his consideration.

However, just three days ago Denise had picked up an unprepossessing, tattered set of school exercise books and she had been tempted to send them back unread for when she opened the top book she saw that the story *A Delightful Scandal* had been handwritten in a childish scrawl which was rather difficult to decipher.

But even as her hand hovered over the pile of rejection slips on her desk, Denise took the trouble to read the first few pages. It was a novel about the sexual experiences of Beverley, a teenage girl in a market town down in the South West of England. It explained how she had first been seduced whilst she was still at school by her history teacher, to her several experiences with boyfriends in the backs of cars and in the boardroom of a local firm of chartered accountants where she was employed as an office girl but in fact, as she candidly confessed, she spent a great deal of time sucking the senior partner's prick. The beautiful Beverley enjoyed flaunting her sensuality and adored having men scramble at her feet for sexual favours and, unlike most good-time girls, at the end of the novel she ends up happily married to a rich Latin-American playboy.

The novel needed polishing up by a good copy-editor, but Denise thoroughly enjoyed reading *A Delightful Scandal* and perhaps because she was herself bi-sexual, was much aroused both by Beverley's uninhibited descriptions of her lovers and by the racy saloon-bar gossip of her boyfriends which alternated with her story.

She had worked extra hours typing out the first five thousand words herself, and had marched into George Radlett's office and passed them to him with a covering memo saying that in her opinion this novel had great possibilities for a mass market sale. Later that day George had called her back into his office and had congratulated her on seeing the potential in *A Dangerous Scandal*.

'It's pretty hot stuff though, Denise, and we all know what our beloved managing director is like when it comes to anything saucy,' he remarked. 'Nevertheless, I've given

Lawrence the extract you typed and recommended that we make an offer to publish a new and certain-to-be-reviewed young British writer.'

Denise mulled over his words as she lay in bed looking at the still slumbering Jenny who had lived with her for the past three months. Young Jenny would also dislike Lawrence, for she was a free-spirited girl and the old Edwardian ephitet of 'prig' would best describe C and P's managing director Lawrence Meade-Richardson who, after taking a law degree at Oxford, had decided not to practise but to join Chelmsford and Parrish, which he was free to do because his maternal grandfather had been a Chelmsford and owned sixty per cent of the company.

Lawrence soon proved himself to be a good salesman and later showed he had the ability to understand the financial complexities of publishing – but he could never rid himself of a starched, patronising manner which irritated many C and P employees. Yet what really annoyed Denise and all the other members of the editorial team was that although Lawrence railed against 'the promiscuity of the present day' in letters to *The Book-seller*, this did not prevent him telephoning his wife to say he would be late home as he had an important book to read, when almost everyone in the firm knew that in fact he was fucking Paula Nayland, the luscious, big-breasted art director, on the lush green carpet in his office.

He was due to deliver his judgement at a nine-thirty meeting this morning and Denise wanted to be there to help George Radlett press the case for publishing *A Delightful Scandal* if, as she expected, Lawrence wanted to veto the book.

Just thinking about some of Beverley's adventures made Denise feel randy and she glanced for a third time at the clock. There was still ten minutes and so she had time for a quick cuddle with Jenny, the lithe eighteen-year-old girl who was now stirring beside her.

Denise gently pulled back the eiderdown and contemplated the glories of Jenny's naked body, from her sweet little nose and generous kissable lips to her thrusting, uptilted young breasts to the curly perfumed hair that framed her pouting pussy lips and which was only a shade or two darker than the silky long strands of blonde hair which framed the head-turning beauty of her face.

The teenager smiled and gave a low, sleepy gurgle of satisfaction as she shifted her position to allow Denise to slip a pillow underneath her so that the mound of her pussy was thrust prominently forward into the bright luminous sunshine which was now playing upon the voluptuous furled lips of Jenny's labia. Denise slid a questing hand over the smooth skin of her stomach and then along the fleshy curve of her hip before dipping downwards to the welcoming vee of Jenny's entrancing sexual junction.

'Oooh, you are naughty, you're making me all wet,' Jenny murmured as Denise rubbed her fingers along the length of her pouting pussy lips.

'I should hope so too,' replied Denise hoarsely as she began to dip her forefinger in and out of Jenny's moistening honeypot. She swung herself round and laid her head on Jenny's thigh as she continued to finger-fuck the younger girl's cunny. 'My word, your pussy has such a succulent scent! What a juicy girl you are, darling! Just look how my finger is getting sucked into your nice wet cunt – wow, if I were a man I'd shaft you with my hot, rigid tool and fuck you till you came all over my cock!'

Like Denise, Jenny Forsyth was also bi-sexual and the imagery of a hard, throbbing prick made her feel even more horny as Denise now started to kiss her tingling mound. She looked down to see Denise's head bobbing between her thighs, her tongue flicking and teasing Jenny's erect clitty which was pushing through her cunny lips like a miniature cock, wallowing in the taste of her love juices as Jenny swiftly exploded into a shuddering, all-embracing orgasm.

The girls then changed positions and Denise now lay flat on her back whilst Jenny licked and lapped her rubbery red nipples whilst she frigged her friend's pussy with her hand. This set off a series of electric pulses racing through Denise's body and her bottom wriggled from side to side on the sheet as Jenny's index finger was now joined by a second and then a third dipping in and out of her sopping love channel.

Jenny moved up over her and, still keeping her fingers embedded in Denise's cunt, kissed her fervently on the lips. Then she withdrew her hand and the two girls rubbed their bodies together, their pubic bushes matting whilst they held each other as tightly as possible. The sheet was soon soaked with their cuntal fluids when after a little sequence of passionate yelps the trembling girls clung to each other as they came off together in a glorious simultaneous climax.

Although Denise would have liked nothing better than to continue this sensual activity, preferably with the new thick dildo which had arrived yesterday from one of her former lovers who was now living in New York, with a note saying that this model had been made from a plaster cast of John Lennon's penis.

Unfortunately, this was not possible because she wanted to be at work before her usual starting time of half past nine, which meant she would have only an hour to shower, dress and make herself some breakfast. So she gave Jenny one final kiss on her shoulder and hauled herself out of bed.

She slipped on a shower-cap and then stood in the

shower, letting the warm water cascade over her body as she wondered how Lawrence Meade-Richardson could be persuaded to publish *A Delightful Scandal*. Of course she would benefit if C and P brought out the novel but, as Denise said to herself as she rehearsed how she might counter Lawrence's objections, she was genuinely convinced it would race to the top of the bestsellers' list.

She was so bound up in working out how best to put this point over at the meeting that she did not hear Jenny tiptoe into the bathroom, and she jumped when she felt the girl's pneumatic body press against her back.

'You're thinking about that book you told me about, aren't you?' said Jenny, planting a series of butterfly kisses on Denise's neck. 'Don't worry so much, darling. If your stupid turd of a boss doesn't want to publish, why don't you write to the author and offer to act as her agent and send the script to another publisher? No-one else need ever know, and if the novel's as good as you say it is, someone else will snap it up so at least you'll make a few bob out of it.'

'Smart thinking, lovey,' said Denise, and a ripple of delight surged through her as Jenny began to wash her back, soaping her shoulders, and Denise purred with pleasure when the teenager started to smooth her soapy hands over her wet bottom.

'Stop that, you naughty kitten, I don't have any time for any more loving this morning,' Denise chuckled whilst Jenny ran her fingers from the rear of her pussy up the crevice between her buttocks, working the cake of soap between her bum cheeks.

Reluctantly, Jenny moved away and let Denise finish her shower undisturbed. As she padded out of the bathroom she called out: 'I'm going back to bed for one last little doze. We were stocktaking in the boutique till almost seven o'clock last night so Mr Bailey said that I don't have to be in till ten o'clock today.'

'Lucky old you,' commented Denise as she towelled herself dry. 'If you're a good girl I'll bring you up a cup of tea before I leave.'

Perhaps subconsciously Denise decided to wear her sexiest outfit and from her drawers she picked out a bra with underwired lace half cups which lifted her breasts and thrust forward her nipples, which were barely covered by the soft shiny material. Then she stepped into a pair of white bikini panties and she twirled herself round suggestively before the mirror before shuffling through the dresses hanging in her wardrobe. After some consideration she chose a pale pink angora jumper which moulded itself around her jutting breasts and a matching tight miniskirt through which the rounded cheeks of her bottom were clearly delineated.

'Hey, talk about dressed to kill,' remarked Jenny when Denise came back to the bedroom with the promised cup of tea. 'Old Lawrence will be so busy trying to hide his hard-on that he won't have time to object to *A Delightful Scandal*.'

Denise grinned and blew the girl a good-bye kiss before hurrying out to the Underground, which she disliked, but the traffic made a journey by bus impossibly slow. On the other hand, the service on the Bakerloo Line was often erratic and there was sometimes a hold-up at Baker Street, but this morning Denise only had time to scan the headlines of the newspaper she bought at the stall on the platform before a Southbound train thundered into the station. She even managed to grab a seat in a non-smoking carriage and although she had to change at Piccadilly Circus for another train to take her to Green Park, by five past nine she was walking into the Georgian building opposite Brown's Hotel in Albemarle Street where Chelmsford and Parrish was housed.

She sat at her desk opening the day's mail when her concentration was broken by a low wolf-whistle from behind her. She turned round and frowned at one of the senior editors, a brash young American named Murray Lupowitz who was working on a exchange scheme with C and P's Jeremy Nolan who was spending twelve months with Murray's employer, a leading New York publisher.

'Who's the lucky guy?' demanded Murray cheerfully. 'No-one, but no-one dresses for work like that if they're not planning to hit the high spots in the evening. Where's he taking you, Denise, a fashionable restaurant, the theatre, or maybe one of these new discotheques where you'll boogie the night away till the early hours.'

Other girls in the company found Murray too free-and-easy, but Denise liked the wise-cracking New Yorker who she'd discovered was exactly two days older than her when on an autumnal Thursday afternoon last year, one of the editorial secretaries brought in a birthday cake for her at tea-time. Before the end of the day, a be-ribboned bottle of champagne from Murray was sitting in her in-tray with a hand-written offer to go out to celebrate their joint birthdays.

Alas, she was unable to accept his invitation as she had arranged to go out to dinner with Jenny, and the next week she again refused the chance to go with him to the cinema. After this second refusal, much to Denise's regret – for although she lived with Jenny, she still enjoyed the company of men – Murray had never asked her out again although they had remained good friends inside the office.

So Denise was not offended by Murray's brashness and she chuckled and shrugged her shoulders as she remarked: 'I'm afraid you're way off base, Yankee Doodle. Believe it or not, I don't have a date tonight.'

'I just don't believe it,' he exclaimed, clapping his hand to his cheek in horror. 'Are there no red-blooded Britons left in Swinging London? My God, if I thought I was in with a chance, I'd ask you out myself.'

He clicked his fingers and went on: 'Hey, that's got to be the very best idea I'll have today! Yeah, how about it, my beautiful English rose? Either we'll celebrate the forthcoming publication of that masterpiece you dredged out of the slush pile, or we'll commiserate together and spend the evening sticking pins in a wax doll of that stupid asshole who has the nerve to call himself a publisher.'

'Do you really mean that?' she asked and Murray nodded vigorously. Then looking around to make sure there was no-one else in the vicinity, he took a couple of quick paces towards her and looked steadily into her large blue eyes.

'Sure I mean it,' he said quietly as he placed his palms on her desk and brought his face even nearer to hers. 'Denise, I don't want to come on heavy but after you gave me a double no-no, I landed myself in a relationship with a nice girl who writes for the *Guardian* diary, who came along to that party we threw for Abigail Jontie's new novel soon after our birthdays.

'That's why I never tried my luck a third time, as I was pretty much involved with this lady,' he continued softly. 'But now that she and I have decided to call it a day, I hope you won't say no to me again.'

Denise heard herself say: 'Thank you, Murray, I won't say no again. I'd very much like to go out with you this evening.'

The American's boyish face lit up and he grabbed her wrist and planted a large smack of a kiss on her hand. 'You've made my day, Miss Cochran! May I suggest a drink at Rodery's Bar after work and then on to a marvellous French restaurant for dinner.'

'I'll look forward to it,' she replied promptly. 'Now, let's hope and pray that we enjoy this morning's meeting as much as I know we'll enjoy ourselves tonight!'

'You know you'll have my support,' said Murray and he kissed her hand again just before George Radlett poked his head round the door and said: 'Ah, I've been looking for you two. Okay, troops, are you ready for battle? Lawrence is waiting for us in the boardroom.'

Denise got up and brushed some imaginary specks from her skirt. She picked up the file on *A Delightful Scandal* and gave George a smart salute. 'Victory or death,' she declared as she and Murray Lupowitz followed their boss up the staircase.

At least the managing director is in a good mood, said Denise to herself as he wished them all a hearty good-morning, and he gave his approval to the first set of editorial plans on the agenda with little comment. This was most surprising for with only a cursory grumble from Lawrence about greedy agents, Murray was given the green light to bid a further seven hundred and fifty pounds to secure the rights to an American novel for which Chelmsford and Parrish had first refusal. Then Lawrence immediately agreed to George Radlett's proposal to foil any other publishers who were keen to sign up C and P's top thriller writer by commissioning three new books from him with a hefty three thousand pounds advance.

Now it was Denise's turn and she brought out her initial report on *A Delightful Scandal* from her file and decided not to beat about the bush but plunge directly into the attack. 'Well, I've circulated my report and a short extract from this novel to one and all. *A Delightful Scandal* comes from the slush pile and it's a jolly romp, extremely racy and probably autobiographical, written by a lady named Erica Boleyn who comes from a little village in Essex.

'The manuscript needs a fair amount of work before publication, but I am certain that it has tremendous possibilities. The novel gives one of the most honest portrayals of female sexuality I have ever read. And yes, it's very rude in places and perhaps we may have to tone down some of the bedroom scenes, but I don't see any reason why we shouldn't have the book ready for publication in late autumn in time for the Christmas market. I believe that the novel would create such a stir that we would sell thousands of copies as well as making a very profitable paperback sale next year. So I recommend making Miss Boleyn an offer of an advance of three hundred pounds on the usual terms, including an option on her next novel.'

Denise sat back and looked around the table at her colleagues. If the meeting were run on a democratic show of hands, there was no doubt she would easily win the day. For Denise knew she could count on the votes of George Radlett and Murray Lupowitz whilst Clive Haverstock, the sales director and Freddie Langley, the publicity manager, would also back her judgement. However, a majority of the votes would not suffice and all would depend on whether Lawrence Meade-Richardson would choose to use his managing director's power of veto.

Murray jumped in immediately to support her, saying that if the company purchased the world rights, he was sure that there would be a clutch of American publishers falling over themselves to buy the rights from Chelmsford and Parrish. George Radlett also spoke in favour of buying the book, as did Clive Haverstock, who was extremely keen to have such a commercial book in the run-up to Christmas which accounted for such a large percentage of the company's sales.

There was a brief silence broken only by the drumming of Lawrence Meade-Richardson's fingers on the polished rosewood table. Then he cleared his throat and said: 'Denise, everyone else seems to be happy to proceed with this novel so it appears that I must act alone as the devil's advocate.

'Yes, I must admit that the book is readable, and I daresay it will attract a great deal of publicity. But leaving aside for the moment any consideration of whether or not we *should* publish such an explicit work, would our lawyers judge it to be obscene? And Clive, I wonder whether the bookshops would be prepared to stock it, especially if one or two of the newspapers climb onto their high horses about fifth and depravity.'

'We might have a problem with one or two of the more crusty booksellers,' admitted Clive Haverstock, 'but since the *Fanny Hill* fiasco four years ago, no-one's going to prosecute us, though it would help sales no end if one or two town councils tried to ban the book!'

'Maybe it would, and maybe it wouldn't, but I can't ignore the fact that there is a great deal of material here which worries me,' said the managing director, wagging a reproving finger at his staff. 'For instance, look at page fourteen of Denise's extract where there's a very raunchy description by the narrator of how she watched her best friend perform oral sex with her boyfriend.'

'I'm afraid I don't have my copy to hand,' said Clive Haverstock, omitting to mention that he had given it to his secretary to see if it would put her in the mood for some rumpy-pumpy at the southern area sales conference which was due to take place that evening at a country hotel in Surrey.

'Oh dear, well I hardly like to read it out loud to you,' said Lawrence doubtfully, but Denise immediately said: 'I don't mind reading it to Clive. On page fourteen, did you say, Lawrence?' She riffled through the pages and went on: 'Ah yes, I've found it. Beverley was walking home one evening through the village green when she heard a noise and peering round a tree she saw her friend petting with one of the boys at school. Then it goes on: *Sharon smacked her lips as she massaged Reggie's erection. Kevin Pearce had shown me how to toss him off so watching Sharon give hand relief to Reggie was nothing new. What did surprise me though was seeing Sharon smack her lips and then lean forward and take his big red knob in her mouth as she cupped his balls in her hands.*

*'I'd read about oral sex but I'd never actually done it so I stayed to watch Sharon lick Reggie's straining shaft, pressing her cheek against it before letting strands of hair fall over his bell-end. She made a web around it, stroking his balls as she moved her head across his helmet and kissed it.*

*' "Urrgh!" groaned Reggie as Sharon opened her mouth wide, closing her lips around his cock. Then she began to bob her head up and down, sucking noisily on the fleshy lollipop as his hands pressed down upon her head as if he feared she might stop, although he need not have worried as it was obvious that Sharon was enjoying herself hugely. Reggie groaned again as she finished him off with gusto, gulping down his emission with relish.*

*'As I watched her gobble Reggie's prick, I wondered whether I would like doing that to Kevin's cock – as I said, this sex play was new to me for I'd wanked Kevin and he'd played with my pussy with his fingers but he had never even suggested that I kiss his cock and—'*

'Thank you, Denise, that's more than enough,' Lawrence interrupted her with some slight irritability in his voice. 'I rest my case. We cannot permit any of our books to be published containing such coarse description of a perverted sexual act. Not only is it far too uninhibited, in any case, I find it quite unbelievable that any girl of seventeen could even think about such things let alone write about them!'

No-one, including Lawrence, had seen the door open whilst Denise had been reading but now the strident tone

of Paula Nayland, C and P's art director who designed the
company's book jackets, filled the room.

'Utter balderdash, Lawrence!' she said in her stentorian
voice which always reminded Denise of Miss Cuthbertson,
her hockey mistress at West Royston Grammar School for
Girls. 'Wake up, man, this is 1967 and except for a few
raddled old fuddy-duddies, no-one thinks of oral sex as
perverted. I know that *I* don't!'

This caused him to blush and the other listeners to
suppress their smiles because all of them knew of the
liaison between Lawrence and the buxom artist. Lawrence
pulled himself together and gave a glassy smile before
making a token stand against his dominating mistress.

'Perhaps so, Paula,' he said feebly, 'but surely a
seventeen-year-old girl would hardly know about such
things.'

'You must be joking,' she snorted contemptuously.
'Why, these days I doubt if even half the sixteen-year-old
girls in London are still virgins. And I say good luck to
them, so long as they or their boyfriends take the necessary precautions not to add further to this over-populated
planet!'

She pulled up a chair and sat down. 'I'm sorry I'm late
but one of my printers wanted me to check some proofs
and there were a couple of changes which needed to be
made. Still, I'm glad I came in before Lawrence kicked *A
Delightful Scandal* into touch. I don't know about everyone else, but I thoroughly enjoyed the extract Denise sent
round. It will really put us on the map and in my not very
humble opinion we would be stark raving mad not to give
it a whirl. Spend a few bob on advertising, Lawrence, it
won't break the bank. Now is there anyone who disagrees
with me?'

Everyone except Lawrence hastily gave their support
and faced with such implacable opposition from Paula,

who had recently been cagey about continuing with their affair, the managing director caved in. 'Very well, I see that I'm outnumbered,' he said grumpily. 'But on your heads be it if I prove to have been right. We'll all have to forget about any Christmas bonuses, that's for sure!'

Nobody was foolish enough to crow over his change of heart but after the meeting Murray pumped Denise's hand and said: 'Well done! I never thought we'd get him to pass it through!'

'Don't thank me, thank Paula,' said Denise and along with George Radlett she went across to express her gratitude personally to her.

Paula waved away their appreciation for her lively comment. 'I only said what I thought,' she said roundly before she marched back to her studio at the very top of the building. 'Lawrence isn't as bad a bloke as some of you might think, but he can be an old stick-in-the-mud at times. So now and then he needs to be shaken out of his complacency by a jolly good shove in the forward direction.'

George Radlett grinned as he gathered up his papers and said: 'She's quite a character, isn't she? Oh, before I forget, Denise, can you please come with me to my office for a couple of moments?'

'Don't settle for less than another thousand a year and a car,' quipped Murray as he held open the door for them and then disappeared down the corridor to his book-lined room.

Denise followed her boss to his spacious office where he ordered coffee for them and, after his secretary had brought in two steaming mugs on a tray, he said to her: 'I'm really pleased, you know, that we'll be publishing your book.'

'It's not my book,' she pointed out with a small smile.

'Erica Boleyn wrote it. All I did was to rescue it from oblivion.'

'Well, you'll do more than that before we publish,' he remarked, passing one of his precious Tottenham Hotspur mugs signed by the great double team of the early sixties to her, for along with his passion for literature, opera and the arts in general, George Radlett was a fanatical football fan and had been offered trials by several professional clubs after he had scored four goals for his local club in an F.A. Amateur Cup tie.

'As you said at the meeting, *A Delightful Scandal* needs quite a lot of editorial work to knock the book into shape and I'd like you to take charge of this project. Carolyn Caughey will advise you about all the financial and legal details of our offer to Erica Boleyn. She's as smart as any lawyer when it comes to drawing up a contract, but she's too tied-up with her own books to help you out on any editorial problems.

'So I spoke to Murray and he said that if asked, he would be delighted to offer an occasional helping hand. He's a clever lad and he can give you a masculine slant on any ideas you might have which might be useful with a novel like this. But do you think you'll be able to work with him?'

Denise was more than happy to agree to such an arrangement and she answered immediately: 'Oh yes, Murray and I seem to get on well together and if it's okay with him, it's okay with me – and thank you very much for giving me this chance to prove myself. It's very kind of you, George, and I appreciate it.'

He raised his hand in protest and continued: 'Not at all, you thoroughly deserve a chance to show your mettle and I'm really pleased we managed to scrape the book by Lawrence at the meeting. Between you and me, we don't have as strong an autumn list as we had last year and I'm relying on *A Delightful Scandal* to give a much-needed boost to the old firm's turnover.

'The book will be your baby, Denise, but obviously I'll want to be given regular progress reports on how things are going. It's quite a tough baptism but if all goes as well as I expect, in a few months time I'd like you to enrol on a business management course at a summer school.'

These last words puzzled Denise but before she could enquire why she needed to study such a subject, George Radlett went on: 'You've probably realised by now that being an editor isn't just sitting around a table discussing the literary merits of this or that author. These days we are hands-on business executives able to make sense of balance sheets and draw up profit and loss charts for each individual book, keeping a tight control of expenses, working out the best way to maximise profits and keeping an eye on the old cash-flow.

'So I want you – and Murray Lupowitz, by the way, who was very keen to go – to take a fortnight's intensive course at a college in Falmington-on-Sea. The tutor will be a chap called Bruce Teplin from the London School of Economics and his first lecture will be on August 4th. We'll pay the fees and take care of all your living expenses. Falmington's a charming little resort with several hotels, though the holiday industry is down in the dumps these days because of all these cheap charter flights to Italy and Spain, so we won't have any problem getting you decent accomodation. I know you might have already made some holiday plans for August and I'm not forcing you to go, but if you'll take my advice you'll go with Murray to Falmington this summer. I'll need a decision by the end of the week.

'Mark my words, Denise,' he concluded in an avuncular fashion. 'What you learn there will stand you in very good stead career-wise whether or not you decide to stay with Chelmsford and Parrish.'

She carefully digested the contents of his little speech and although she had talked about spending some time on a Greek island with Jenny in August, she realised that she would be foolish to turn down this offer. So she replied: 'George, I can tell you now that I'll go to Falmington with Murray. As you say, it's a great opportunity for me to learn more about the job.'

'Good show, I'm sure you won't regret it,' said George Radlett with great satisfaction. 'I'll enrol you both this afternoon.'

Denise finished her coffee and went back to her office where she began making some preliminary drafts of a letter to Erica Boleyn which won the approval of Carolyn Caughey who also suggested she might like to call the author and give her the good news over the telephone.

'Hopefully, this will give you the chance to establish a friendly personal relationship, which will be important if you'll be editing her book,' explained the senior editor.

Unfortunately there was no reply from Miss Boleyn's telephone number and Denise made a note to try again the next day. Meanwhile there was plenty of other work to get through before half past five when Murray would come to call for her.

At five-thirty-three Murray Lupowitz was standing in front of her desk and reminding her that all overtime was unpaid and ten minutes later they were sitting down at a table by the window inside Rodney's, one of the most fashionable of the smart new wine bars which were fast establishing themselves in the West End. A waiter set two glasses of dry white wine in front of them and Murray picked up his glass and said: 'Well, my little upward bound one, who should we toast first this evening? Paula Nayland? Or even our beloved Lawrence M-R?'

'You're as bad as George Radlett, Murray. I had to remind him that it was Erica Boleyn's contribution which made everything possible,' she mildly scolded him. 'Let's drink to *A Delightful Scandal*, long may it top the bestseller lists.'

'Fair enough, here's to Erica and her naughty novel,' he grinned and they clinked their glasses together and toasted their budding new author.

She put down her glass and said: 'I understand that George has already spoken to you about the two of us going back to school in August. I'll be taking a course in business management. Will you be in my class?'

Murray shook his head sadly. 'Uh-uh, I majored in business studies at Yale. No, I want to take a crash course in Spanish. The powers that be in the firm I work for back home already own publishing houses in Argentina and Mexico and next year they plan to open up in Madrid, because not even Franco can last for ever and when he dies or is finally forced out there'll be a great opportunity to publish all the great books the old bastard won't let into the country. I've a personal reason to help that project get off the ground because I have an uncle who lost an arm fighting in the International Brigade during the Spanish Civil War.

'But that was thirty years ago and what's past is past. I've been over to Madrid and Barcelona and everyone there is waiting for Franco to kick the bucket when they'll be able to rejoin the twentieth century. I'll probably have to unlearn the bits and pieces of the Spanish I've already picked up in New York from a Puerto Rican guy I know, but I'm looking forward to learning the language properly at this summer school.'

Denise listened to him with interest for this was the first time she had heard the easy-going young American speak so seriously and she commented: 'Yes, I can see why you want to learn Spanish, Murray, but truthfully, I don't understand why Lawrence Meade-Richardson of all people would agree to pay for your course!'

'A very good question, and the short answer is that he's not, I'm paying for myself,' declared Murray with a wry chuckle. 'My employment with Chelmsford and Parrish finishes in August and instead of flying back to the States straight away, I've decided to stay in England for another three weeks so I can enrol at Falmington.'

His reply surprised Denise and she asked: 'Why did you do that? Surely you'd learn much more by going over to Spain and living there during August.'

Murray bit his lip and looked down shyly at his half-empty glass as he spoke. 'I guess there are three reasons why I'm staying here, if I'm to give you an honest answer.

'Firstly, this summer school comes highly recommended – I know some people at London University and they've told me the courses at Falmington are just about the best of their kind in Britain. For instance, you'll have Bruce Teplin as your lecturer and his book *The Basics Of Management* was on the reading list when I was at college. I don't know who my tutor will be but whoever it is will be an expert linguist, that's for sure. Secondly, you know I'm a gregarious guy, Denise, I love company and I think I'd be very lonely in a big foreign city where I don't even speak the language. And in August it's so damned hot that lots of people our age take their vacations and I could see myself sitting alone in my hotel room every evening.'

Murray paused and Denise said softly: 'And what's the third reason?'

'You,' he said simply and a pink blush suffused his cheeks as he placed his elbows on the table and rested his chin in his hands. 'When George Radlett mentioned that he was sending you to Falmington I decided then and there that I would book in there as well.'

Denise thought quickly as she brushed back the strands of silky, strawberry blonde hair which had tumbled over her face. She was definitely attracted to this slim, good-looking young American but it had been almost a year since she had slept with anyone but a woman. It was not that Denise was repelled by the thought of sharing her bed with a man, far from it, but her last lover had deceived her cruelly by suddenly leaving one day with no prior warning, and shortly afterwards she discovered that not only had he stolen money from her wallet but that for the past few months he had also been carrying on a clandestine affair with one of her so-called best chums.

She felt that she could not trust any man again after so much hurt and as she had always enjoyed her previous brief lesbian flings, Denise decided that she would prefer to give men a miss. Yet whilst she had loved the passionate love making with Jenny Forsyth, there was no doubt that she had missed the driving force of a man during their sexual encounters.

'A penny for your thoughts,' said Murray, reaching out to caress her hand with his long, slender fingers. 'I hope this confession hasn't spoiled the evening for you.'

'No, of course not,' said Denise, rising from her seat for she had decided not to hold back if at the end of the evening she wanted to be fucked by this genuinely nice man. 'Murray, I'll be back in a minute but I just must make a quick 'phone call.'

The barman directed her to the telephone and fortunately Jenny was still at their flat. 'Jenny, I forgot that one of the people here is giving a party tonight and it would look stand-offish if I don't show up. But it's way out of town somewhere in Hertfordshire so I'll be back very late – or I might even stay over.'

'Okay, no problem, it's not that we had anything arranged and anyhow I have to go back to the shop and finish the stocktaking,' said her flat-mate. 'But tell me, how did the meeting go? Did you get your way with that stupid bugger, Lawrence?'

'Yes, it was great! He didn't want to publish it but everyone was against him and in the end he backed down,' replied Denise, who felt bad about not telling Jenny the real reason why she was not coming straight home. On the other hand, she had a vague suspicion that Jenny too might harbour sensual feelings for a member of the opposite sex, in particular the older but craggily handsome Mr Bailey who owned the boutique (along with three others in the West End of London) where Jenny worked as a salesgirl.

When she returned to their table, a jazz combo was playing at the far end of the bar and Murray and Denise decided to spend the rest of the evening at Rodney's which boasted a postage stamp dance floor and also offered a small but well-prepared supper menu.

'But next time you must let me take you to *La Garonne*, this new French restaurant I was telling you about,' Murray insisted and he snapped his fingers and added: 'Hold on a minute, I'd better cancel the booking I made for tonight, it's only fair.'

'We'll see,' she said guardedly, but by the end of the evening she would have answered positively without hesitation. As they ate their dinner, they talked freely about their lives, although Denise never mentioned her current lesbian love affair with Jenny. They relished each other's company so much that time flew by and Denise was quite astounded when the barman called for last orders shortly before eleven o'clock.

She knew that the moment of truth was fast approaching for when they had smooched cheek to cheek on the dance floor, she had felt Murray's rock-hard erection pressing firmly against her tummy. What should she do if

Murray asked her back to his flat for a night-cap? It would be wanton to go further than a chaste good-night kiss on a first date, but Denise was hungry for more than a touch of his lips and she knew that if they proceeded further than that, she would be unable to resist any further advances.

Sure enough, Murray asked the fateful question whilst they waited for the waiter to bring back his American Express card. 'Time to order a cab, love. I only live less than ten minutes away in Exhibition Road. Let me make you some coffee there and then I'll drive you back to St John's Wood.'

'Well, it's a bit late for coffee, we both have to go to work in the morning,' she said doubtfully, but it was when Murray wrapped his arm around her as they sat in the back seat of the taxi and she experienced a delightful warm tingling in her groin that Denise decided to accept his invitation.

The taxi dropped them outside a smart block of luxury flats and as the uniformed porter opened the door and wished them good evening, Denise muttered: 'Murray, are you moonlighting or have you won the pools? No-one could afford to live here on the kind of pittance that we're paid.'

'True enough, but fortunately an English friend of our family built these flats and he gave me this apartment at a very low rent,' he admitted as he unlocked the front door and ushered Denise into the hall. 'Now what will you have, coffee, tea or me?'

She laughed out loud at his forthright question and said: 'My God, I never realised you were such a subtle guy! Still, I suppose there's nothing like getting straight to the point!'

He helped Denise slip off her coat and then from behind her, Murray slid his arm around her waist and gently nibbled her earlobe as he said lightly: 'Well, you know what the British used to say about us Yanks during the war – we're over-fed, over-sexed and over here!'

He spun her round and drew her close to him. He kissed her cheeks, nose and ears and then their mouths met. Despite some initial pangs of doubt, Denise found her body responding as they held each other and rocked quietly whilst the warmth of passion turned into burning hot desire deep inside her.

Without breaking their kiss, Murray gathered her up in his arms and she clung to him with her arms locked about his neck as he walked through into his bedroom and deposited her softly upon the mattress.

'Denise, you are so lovely,' he murmured, tenderly sweeping the hair from her face, and when his fingers released the fastener at the top of her jumper she raised her arms and he pulled it over her shoulders whilst she kicked off her shoes. He was so excited that he fumbled clumsily with the clasps of her bra, but Denise was now also carried away by the fire which was raging inside her entire body and she reached back herself and undid the hooks for him, baring her beautiful breasts which he cupped in his hands.

The surrounding silence was broken only by their swift, shallow breaths as Denise now took the initiative and pulled his head to the taut, elongated nipples of her jutting breasts and he licked and lapped at the rubbery red morsels whilst she arched her back upwards to allow him to roll her panties and tights down over her feet.

For a fleeting instant Murray looked with undisguised craving at her luscious nudity and then, whilst he ripped off his clothes she watched with a growing appetite and, when he tugged down his Y-fronts, she caught her breath sharply as she saw the stiff, swollen shaft of his circumcised penis standing up proudly against his stomach.

Murray moved swiftly to the bed to crouch above her, brushing her lips with a butterfly kiss whilst his knee nestled between her thighs and his hand slid downwards to revel in the soft, furry feel of her silky bush. Then he kissed her breasts again, switching his attentions from one juicy nipple to the other and she moaned with delight as he moved his head downwards across the flat whiteness of her tummy, licking around her belly-button before finding its way to her damp curls of pubic hair.

He parted her pussy lips with two fingers, feasting his eyes on the glowing red chink of her cunt, the aromatic, delicate flow of honey and the pretty strands of wet hair curling around his fingers as he dipped them inside her juicy love channel. She moaned as he slid his hands under Denise's adorably rounded buttocks and lifted her crack to his waiting mouth, but her moan changed to a satisfied purr when he kissed the soft, pouting lips at the entrance of her cunny and began to lick along them, and her entire body writhed with excitement whilst the tip of Murray's tongue sought out the secrets of her sopping slit.

'Aaagh! Aaagh!' she panted as her clitty popped out from its shell as he tickled it with his darting tongue and her tangy love liquid flowed over his face. Murray gleefully inhaled the pungent aroma which acted as an aphrodisiac as he brought off the trembling girl with his tongue, sucking her clitty until she shrieked with joy as she achieved her climax.

Denise was now so excited that as the delicious tingling warmth died away, she grabbed hold of his rampant prick and rubbed the smooth, stiff shaft up and down until she could feel it pulse between her fingers.

'Fuck me, Murray, I want to feel your lovely thick joystick inside me,' she told him and she held his cock tightly as he raised himself on top of her and she closed her eyes and sighed with joy as he guided his cock deep into her squishy wetness.

Their bodies were soon joined from mouth to groin as

Murray's hairy chest crushed against her breasts whilst he pistoned his prick in and out of her clinging honeypot. He thrust his stiff truncheon inside her up to the hilt, his balls lying against the backs of her thighs, delighting in the feel of her cunny muscles tightening on his sinewy shaft.

'Oh, I'm so *full*!' gasped Denise as she crossed her legs over the small of his back. 'Now fuck me, you randy boy! Let me feel that big cock slither in and out of my juicy cunt!'

'Okay, you got it,' he growled and slowly jerked his hips back and forth as he began to fuck her with long, sensuous strokes. 'But you must tell me how I should finish? Can I come inside you?'

The thought flashed wildly through Denise's mind that she must have known she really wanted to be fucked by a man again when two months ago she had decided to go back on the pill, and her heart warmed yet more towards Murray for remembering to pose this important question even at this final stage.

'Yes! Yes! Yes!' she breathed fiercely, and Murray smiled as she saw her eyes shine with desire and he whispered: 'Then hold me tight, Denise my darling, here we go!'

The American jammed his shaft forward, burying it once more to the root which made Denise shriek loudly as her body bucked with delight as his shaft sank thrillingly home. Then he began to fuck her with style, his lean bum cheeks rising and falling in a quickening rhythm, leading them both swiftly towards the pinnacle of pleasure.

Murray rubbed his palms against her raised-up nipples whilst he plunged his prick in and out of her dripping love funnel, his balls banging against her bottom as his body quivered in anticipation of the oncoming orgasm which he knew could no longer be delayed. Murray groaned as the sweet warmth of his climax suffused every fibre of his being and he surrendered himself to the joy of the moment, shooting his creamy jism into Denise's willing cunt as her lithe body twisted and writhed underneath him with the force of her own tremendous orgasm.

Slowly he pulled his cock out of her soaking pussy and to her delight, Denise could see that his shaft was still hard. She slicked her hand around his tadger and pulled his prick towards her lips. She licked off the coating of their juices from his helmet and then, taking his knob inside her soft, mobile mouth, Denise caressed it firmly with her lips and tongue, sending further shockwaves of intense sensuality throughout Murray's frame, thrilling his senses with intense passion.

To Murray's surprise, as her magic tongue travelled wetly along his tool and her teeth scraped the tender underside of his knob, he soon felt his balls hardening a second time and he ejaculated again, filling her mouth with his frothy spunk which she gulped down until his cock lost its stiffness and she released his limp organ from between her lips.

He moved his body off her to lie by her side, pulling the duvet over them before cradling her in his arms. She looked at him lovingly and said: 'Was it as good for you as it was for me?'

Murray chuckled softly and replied: 'Hey, that's my line! I know this is Swinging London but isn't it still up to the man to enquire if he needs to do more to make sure his lady is satisfied?'

'Times change, m'dear,' she twinkled as she snuggled herself into the crook of his shoulder and as an image of she and Jenny Forsyth playing with each other came to mind she added: 'And, come to that, so do people. Oh, I'm so comfortable, Murray, I'd love to stay the night and make love with you again when we wake up in the morning but I must get back to my flat.'

'Please don't go now, darling,' he begged her as she slipped out of bed. 'I'll drive us into work tomorrow as George Radlett is spending the day out of the office with Lionel Trippett, that new horror writer he signed up last month, so I can use his space in the parking lot.'

Denise was much tempted but she shook her head and said sadly: 'I'm sorry, Murray, but I must leave. For a start, I need a change of clothes. You don't have to get up, though, I'll call a minicab.'

'You'll do no such thing,' he said sternly as he threw back the duvet and heaved himself up. 'What kind of man do you take me for? Not one of these wham, bam, thank you ma'am types, I hope.'

'No, of course I don't,' she exclaimed, wrapping her arms round his neck and giving him a quick squeeze. 'But it's pretty late to start driving to St John's Wood and back.'

He kissed her forehead as he looked at his watch. 'It's only a quarter to one, you silly girl,' he smiled and he patted her bottom as he went on: 'Now come on, there's time for a quick wash and brush-up before we hit the road.'

There was little traffic as Murray gunned his MGB sports car through the empty streets, and in less than ten minutes they screeched to a halt outside Denise's front door.

He moved across and kissed her on the lips. 'Don't forget we skipped dinner at my favourite French restaurant,' he reminded her. 'If you're free on Friday night—'

'I don't think I am,' she cut in, remembering that she was supposed to go with Jenny to a party being thrown by one of their most outrageous lesbian friends, but added hastily: 'But any other evening should be fine.' They agreed on the following Tuesday night for their dinner at *La Garonne* 'on condition that we take in a movie on

Sunday evening,' said Murray.

'Why not?' Denise smiled and whilst he leaped out of the car and strode round to open her door, she recalled that Jenny had planned to spend Sunday with her parents who lived in Berkshire and wouldn't be back till late on Sunday night. 'But only if you'll let me cook some supper before we go. How does spaghetti bolognese with a bottle of Chianti hit you?'

'Right in the solar plexus! We'll choose the film over a tuna fish salad in my office at lunchtime. My treat. After all, what's the point of having a secretary if she doesn't go out and queue up at the sandwich bar for you,' he quipped as Denise rummaged through her handbag for her keys. When she found them and opened the front door, they embraced briefly and then Murray blew her a kiss and hurried back to his car. Denise watched him roar away before going inside and closing the door behind her.

She decided to undress in the lounge in order not to wake up Jenny. After she had finished, she went into the bathroom and cleaned her teeth. Then she tip-toed naked into the darkened bedroom, but as she slipped quietly into their large double bed, Jenny stirred and murmured drowsily: 'Hello, sweetie-pie, did you have a nice evening?'

'Yes, thank you, I had a really nice time,' she replied and to Denise's surprise, Jenny suddenly sat up and switched on her bedside light.

'Darling, what's the matter? Are you feeling unwell?' she demanded and the teenage girl nodded and brushed silky strands of blonde hair from her pretty face.

'I'm fine, Denise, really I am, but I'm not that sleepy,' she said. 'Unless you're all-in, I'd very much like to talk to you about something that's troubling me.'

Denise glanced at the clock. 'Can't it wait till morning, love? We'll both have to get up early, you know.'

And Now The Girls . . .

'Yes, I know, but I'd be grateful if you'd listen to me for a few minutes 'cos this is important,' Jenny persisted and because she was naturally a kind-hearted girl and as she was still riding high on the excitement of her love-making with Murray, Denise hauled herself up and said: 'All right, Jenny, I can see you must get whatever is bothering you off your chest here and now. Fire away, lovey, I'm all ears.'

Jenny smiled gratefully and said: 'Thanks, Denise, you're a real pal, and that's why I need to tell you about the amazing time I had tonight.'

'The amazing time you had tonight,' Denise repeated, scratching her head in puzzlement. 'But when I telephoned you to say I'd be in late, you told me that you were going back to the boutique to finish your stocktaking.'

'That's right, I only came home to change into my jeans because Mr Bailey and I were also going to clear the basement and I didn't want to get my dress dirty,' she confirmed and Denise commented: 'Well, I'm sorry, Jenny, but that doesn't sound very amazing to me!'

The younger girl giggled and said: 'No, I suppose it doesn't, but that's when it all started.'

'When all *what* started?' demanded Denise. 'I'm afraid I'm not with you.'

'Sorry, I'm not making myself clear,' apologised Jenny. 'I'd better start by confessing something to you. I've rather fancied Mr Bailey ever since I started working at his shop. But till tonight he had always been the perfect gentleman – too bloody perfect, actually – and I know he's never tried his luck with any of the girls.'

'However, tonight was different,' said Denise drily, wondering to herself whether coincidentally Jenny had also sampled the joys of a thick prick between her thighs, which would not have upset her for she knew that like

67

herself, the blonde teenager had enjoyed previous relationships with men.

'Oh, don't worry, you soppy thing, you know very well I'm not the jealous type,' she continued, giving the younger girl an encouraging hug. 'Just give me a blow-by-blow account and don't leave out any of the randy bits!'

Jenny kissed her shoulder and said: 'Thanks again, Popsie, and okay, I'll tell you everything. To be honest, I find it exciting to talk about all the sordid details!'

'Carry on, my love,' invited Denise with a smile. 'How did it all begin?'

'I suppose when Mr Bailey sent Heather home and asked me if I would just help him move the rails of sale dresses to the back of the shop,' replied Jenny.

'The rails aren't heavy but as I pushed mine, I slipped and fell to the floor. Pete, Mr Bailey that is, rushed up and helped me to my feet.

' "Ow!" I cried out as I hobbled to a chair. "I think I've twisted my ankle."

'He was most concerned and suggested that he massaged it. He had a wonderful touch for after a couple of minutes, I told him that my foot was okay again and he said: "Thank God for that, I would have been terribly upset if you had really hurt yourself. Tell you what, Jenny, I'll bet you haven't had any supper yet, have you? Well, neither have I, so let's go round the corner and let me treat you to a meal at Geraldine's."

'This was a smart new bistro which had only just opened and I said: "That's kind of you, but I'm hardly dressed to go out for dinner, am I?"

' "Oh, that doesn't matter," he said, heaving me up to my feet. "Anyhow, look at me, I've also only got jeans on and anyway, the people who go there are very laid back and more than half of them will be wearing jeans as well."

'I was a bit doubtful but I was delighted to be asked so I

agreed and, not only was Pete right about none of the diners dressing up, but the restaurant was not too crowded and we sat at a lovely quiet table for two at the back of the restaurant. The food was scrumptious. I had the chef's special – grilled chicken served with stir-fried vegetables and a ginger, lime and honey sauce. We downed two big carafes of wine and by the time we reached the coffee stage we'd told each other far more about ourselves than in all the time I'd been working for him.'

'And this was roughly when your legs brushed against each other under the table?' suggested Denise with a grin.

'How did you guess?' said Jenny with mock astonishment in her voice. 'I think I told you how I'd been wondering why Pete had not been his usual cheery self over the last few weeks. Well, now he told me that this was because he had finally broken off with the girlfriend who'd been living with him on and off for over a year or so. Then he asked me if I was seeing someone, saying that he always tried to separate business from pleasure and never dated any of the girls who worked in his boutiques, but then in a great rush he said that he fancied me rotten and was finding it hard to keep cool when I was around!

' "Especially when you're wearing one of those figure-hugging mini-dresses, although you look tremendously sexy in those tight jeans," he burst out in a fierce whisper. "And I have to tell you that you must have the most beautifully rounded backside I've ever seen, and believe me, after working in the rag trade for more than ten years, I've clapped eyes on literally hundreds of girls' behinds, bare, beknickered and bejeaned!"

' "You've never seen my bare bottom, so don't be too complimentary about it," I said coyly and, emboldened by the fact that I did not take offence at his remark, Pete went on: "No, but hopefully there'll be an opportunity later tonight to find out. Jenny, I don't beat about the bush and so I'm going to tell you straight out that I fancy you something rotten.

' "It's not fair, I know it isn't, and if you refuse me, I promise that it won't make any difference as far as your prospects at the boutique are concerned, but I have something very important to tell you." '

She paused and then chuckled softly: 'I had more than an inkling of what he was going to say just by looking at the tremendous bulge in his lap but I simply asked: "What might that be, Pete?" and he took a deep breath before replying: "Jenny, more than anything else in the world, I want you to come back to my flat and make mad, passionate love with me." '

Denise gave a short laugh. 'Your Mr Bailey wastes no time in making a bee-line for goal. Still, I like a man who has the guts to come right out and tell you what he wants, and I admire the fact that he had the decency to let you know beforehand that your job wasn't on the line and he wasn't trying to blackmail you into his bed. I'm sure that if you'd have said no he would have been disappointed, but being a gentleman he would have accepted your decision and that would have been the end of the matter.'

Jenny pinched her playfully on the arm. 'Hey, what makes you so sure that I didn't say no?' she demanded and Denise wagged a reproving finger. 'Leave it out, Jenny, if you hadn't gone back to his flat you wouldn't have waited up to tell me this story!'

'Touché, pussycat! Still, I did mull his proposition over for at least fifteen seconds before I agreed to it! Of course, once I'd said I'd go back to his pad, Pete couldn't wait to get out of the restaurant.

'We walked arm in arm to his car and it only took a few minutes to drive to West Hampstead where he lives in a splendid old Edwardian mansion just off Fortune Green which he bought and converted into three apartments.

Pete took the garden flat for himself and I wanted to look around, but as soon as we were inside he swept me into the bedroom and threw his arms around me.

' "Okay, okay, you don't have a train to catch, let me take off my coat," I gasped as he held me in a bear-hug. You've seen Pete before, he's quite a hunk, six foot two and he can't weigh much less than thirteen stone – and he hung his head and apologised. "Sorry, Jenny, I'm just so excited that I couldn't hold myself back."

' "Well I hope you'll be able to hold yourself back once we get properly started," I said, blowing him a kiss. "Now first things first, where's the bathroom?"

'When I came back Pete was sitting on the bed and I don't mind admitting that my pussy was already moist when we put our arms around each other and our mouths came together and dissolved into a passionate kiss. He pushed up my jumper and grunted with delight when he discovered I wasn't wearing a bra, and he fondled my bare breasts, tweaking my nipples until it felt as if they were sticking out like two little red pricks!

'Then he pulled open the top button of my jeans and pulled down the zipper and, still with our lips glued together, he manoeuvred them over my hips and I arched my bum upwards to help him pull them down to the floor. Now there was a very real wetness in my panties and I moved my legs slightly apart as Pete slid his hand inside the top of my knickers and moved his fingers through the damp public hair, downwards along my slit from top to bottom. My pussy was sending out electric waves of delight as his fingers slid up and down, pressing down expertly on my clitty until I was almost on the brink of a cum.

'Ever so gently he laid me down on the bed and I raised my arms and he pulled off my jumper. Now it was my turn to begin undressing him so I sat up and reached for his belt

71

which I unbuckled whilst he tore off his shirt. I unzipped his flies and slipped my hand inside his boxer shorts to bring out his stiffie. And what a beautiful big prick it was, at least eight inches long, and very thick with a big uncapped knob and a pretty blue vein running along his shaft.

'Yes, I know I've often said to you that I didn't ever want to be fucked by a man again after that awful affair with Beresford what's-his-name at the youth club. But any remaining doubts I might have had about having sex with a boy disappeared when I grasped hold of Pete's luscious cock and rubbed my hand up and down its hot, velvet-smooth shaft.

'I lay my head back on the pillow waiting for him to fuck me, but now his initial feverish excitement had worn off and he swung himself between my legs and I shuddered all over as he ran his hands along the inside of my thighs. After he rolled down my panties to my feet and I had kicked them off, I wondered if he was going to lick me out – no man had ever done this to me before and I hoped that Pete would suck my pussy.

'Actually, I knew that he was one of the few men I'd met who were happy to pleasure their lovers this way, because one lunchtime in the pub I'd overheard Sylvia, his former live-in, tell one of the girls who works with me in the boutique that Pete was a marvellous muff-diver. They had been comparing notes on their boyfriends and obviously the other girl's man didn't know how to bring her off with his mouth, but Sylvia had said proudly: "Oh, I'm very lucky 'cos Pete's terrific when it comes to eating pussy. Honestly, I really think he would have won a gold medal if there had been a cunnilingus competition in those Commonwealth Games last year."

'So I encouraged him by spreading my cunny lips with my fingers and sure enough he lowered his head and began licking my thighs and then the tip of his tongue passed over my saturated slit. He looked up at me for a moment and said: "What a gorgeous little cunt you have, Jen, let me just brush aside some of this lovely blonde bush – ah, that's better, now I can kiss your pretty cunny lips." '

'M'mm, it all sounds very exciting,' said Denise whose own pussy was tingling with mounting excitement. 'And was he as good as you'd heard?'

'Is the Pope Catholic, darling! It was so nice that I started to come off almost as soon as Pete nuzzled his mouth against my pussy and whirled his tongue inside my dripping crack. He splayed my cunny lips open with his fingers and sucked on my clitty and rolled his tongue round the most sensitive part whilst he nibbled on it with his teeth. His hands gripped my hips and I twisted from side to side so violently that he found it difficult to keep his mouth on my clit.

'But then I began to spend and he finger-fucked me till my orgasm was over and he finished off by lapping up the love liquid out of my sopping cunt as I cried out with joy. I held his head in my hands, pressing his lips onto my soaking muff and he didn't stop till I had finished, licking me with lovely slow strokes, sucking my pussy whilst I drenched his face with sprays of cunny juice as wonderful waves of pleasure spread out from my groin all over my body.

'I kept his face firmly between my thighs as he licked up the last tangy drains of my spend. But after I'd finished, I pulled Pete up until his head was next to mine on the pillow, and feeling grateful perhaps for his marvellous muff-diving, I rolled over on top of his hunky torso, holding tightly on to his rock-hard, pulsating prick.

' "Stay still, lover, it's my turn to do the work," I breathed softly as I heaved myself up and straddled him.

Then still with his stiff cock throbbing away in my hand, I slowly eased myself down upon the big round knob and started to slide rhythmically up and down his pole which was soon nice and wet from my love juices which were still trickling out of my cunt.

' "Is that good for you? Or would you prefer me to stop?" I asked, which was a really silly question because you only had to look at the blissful expression on his face to see that he was enjoying every second of this lovely lazy fuck!

' "No, no, for God's sake don't stop," he cried out and then he opened his eyes wide and grinned broadly. "Jenny Forsyth, you're as randy as I am, you naughty girl!" and he laughed out loud as he rubbed my nipples against the palms of his hand whilst I bounced up and down on his beefy chopper, pumping my bum up and down as I dug my nails into his muscular thighs.

'Pete started to jerk his hips upward in time with my downward thrusts on his twitching tool. He lifted his trunk upwards to suck on my stalky titties and then he stuttered: "Jenny, I'm going to come, can I—"

' "Yes, Yes, Yes! I'm well protected. Shoot off your spunk inside me, you big-cocked boy!" I gasped, and that's just what he did, creaming my cunt with a great fountain of jism which set off my own climax, and ripples of bliss flowed out of my sated cunt.'

Jenny was about to continue but she suddenly looked at Denise and drew in a sharp breath. 'Oh darling, I shouldn't have let Pete Bailey fuck me, I've been unfaithful to you, my best and closest friend.'

'Don't be daft, it all sounds quite wonderful,' said Denise wistfully as she thought of the gorgeous sex she had enjoyed only hours ago with Murray Lupowitz. 'I know what's going through your mind, but there's absolutely no need for you to feel guilty about anything that happened between you and your boss.

'Let's face it, we've both had rotten experiences with men and probably we'll always enjoy an occasional girls-only session, but deep down I think we both know that we don't want to spend the rest of our lives without ever being fucked by a thick meaty cock! No, I mean that, Jenny, I really do, for I knew that something like tonight would happen at some time.

'Listen, I wasn't going to tell you till later, but believe it or not there's been a crazy coincidence. I was also fucked by a fella tonight, that hunky young American lad who I've talked about now and then.'

Jenny looked at her open-mouthed and gasped: 'Denise! You're having me on! You're not just making this up to make me feel better about tonight?'

'Word of honour I'm not, and there's no reason why anything should change until we see which way the wind blows,' insisted Denise, kissing her cheek. 'Perhaps one of us will want to change the sleeping arrangements, but you and I will always be friends, won't we?'

'Of course we will,' cried the younger girl. 'Oh, I feel so happy! And I don't want to stop sleeping with you so long as you want me in your bed. Why shouldn't we both have our cake and eat it?'

Denise patted her shoulder and said: 'Why not indeed, darling, but time will tell. Meanwhile, let's get some sleep.'

# CHAPTER THREE

## *Frolics in Falmington*

In the neat but slightly run-down little town of Falmington-on-Sea on the Sussex coast the month of August opened in a blaze of beautiful sunshine tempered only by the balmiest of sea breezes and, for the first time in several years, Falmington's hapless publicity officer, Bernie Gosling, was able to tell the truth and nothing but the truth when he made his daily telephone call to those national newspapers who carried league tables of the number of sunshine hours in the seaside resorts up and down the country.

Bernie prayed that the fine weather would continue because last year had been little short of disastrous for the hotels and boarding houses, with only one gloriously warm week the entire summer, and that in early July when most of the visitors were old-age pensioners taking advantage of the pre-season cheap rates. The critical weeks of late July and August had been wet and windy, with four of his open-air Sunday concerts having to be cancelled along with the grand charity cricket match which would have brought a gaggle of celebrities to the town, along with some much needed publicity.

These were trying times for Bernie as even members of the town council were divided as to whether to plough more money into a razzmatazz programme of attractions for the 1967 season, or throw in the towel and concentrate their minds on the idea of setting up a commercial park for light industry on the edge of the town and letting the once important holiday trade find its own level.

Naturally, enough, at forty-seven years of age Bernie had no desire to be made redundant and he campaigned vigorously for funds to promote the town's tourist facilities. At countless committee meetings he assured the councillors that given a reasonable budget he could increase the number of summer visitors, although even Mr Amos, the Chairman of the Finance Committee, who himself owned a small hotel on the sea-front, felt uneasy at the thought of throwing more money at what many people believed was an insoluble problem, given the increasing popularity of cheap continental summer holidays.

'Perhaps we should move with the times and give close consideration to the plans submitted by those property developers to build factories and offices by Portland Park,' said Mr Amos, hoping that no-one on the council was aware that his son had owned much of the land where the developers planned to construct the new site.

Fortunately for Bernie, an alliance of old-fashioned Conservative country gentlemen and ecologically conscious anti-capitalist Labour councillors had pushed through an only slightly reduced leisure budget by a vote which was too close for comfort.

So for Bernie, a former feature writer with the old *News Chronicle* who enjoyed life away from London, this would be a make-or-break summer for he had decided to back Andy Swaffer, an enterprising hotelier, who was promoting Falmington to a new crowd of younger families by staging a set of Sunday concerts featuring stars from the popular TV shows.

Hopefully, this would woo holidaymakers away from the lure of Spanish sunshine and Bernie had gambled much of his budget on the publicity for Shane Hammond and the Hurricanes, a hugely popular rock group who were booked to appear on Sunday week at the Queen's Hall. This was a smallish but well-kept theatre owned by the town council and leased during the summer season to Teddy Dixon of the Rose and Griffin agency who every year cobbled together a variety show to run during the summer season, hosted by one of the better-known entertainers on their books and featuring a selection of their 'rising stars', plus a chorus line consisting of dancers who had passed a very private audition on the leather couch in Teddy Dixon's office.

However, although Bernie was confident that Shane Hammond would help pull more people into the town, he realised that he still needed a few weeks of good weather during the season. Not only would this mean that those holidaymakers who had booked up this year would be well-disposed to return to Falmington, but they would also tell their friends – and the lure of the Shane Hammond concerts might well bring in many day trippers which would also benefit the pubs and restaurants on the four Sundays concerned.

A long, hot spell will make all the difference as to whether I'm fired or made a freeman of the town, he muttered to himself as he plumped himself down in the comfortable armchair in his office and started to tackle the first job of the day, which was to glance through all the morning newspapers to see if there were any chances to place the odd story about Falmington in the media.

So Bernie could not be blamed for gloating when he opened his *Daily Mirror* and read that up North torrential rain had brought floods to Yorkshire and Lancashire, and that enormous hailstones 'the size of golf balls' had damaged cars around Macclesfield. With a grunt of satisfaction he heaved himself up and went over to his desk and, after inserting a sheet of paper into his typewriter, he began to draft a news release for the Press Association tapes which would inform any interested, bedraggled Northerners that latecomers could still be accomodated in sunny Falmington, for there were quite a few empty rooms waiting to be filled in the town's hotels and there were still several 'vacancies' signs to be seen in the windows of Falmington's boarding houses.

This should make a good story for the *Yorkshire Post*, he thought as he pounded away on the old manual machine which next year he would trade in for an expensive electric model if all went according to plan during the next four weeks.

The door opened and he looked up to see the nubile figure of Sandie Walters, his attractive young secretary, framed in the doorway. Not for the first time, Bernie wondered whether Sandie dressed in deep-cut blouses and tight mini-skirts just to tease him.

Since Bernie's wife had never settled in Falmington and had finally moved back to London to live with the picture editor of the *Evening Globe*, life had been lonely at times for the publicist, especially since his two sons had also left home, one bound for America to work in computers for IBM and the other up to Scotland where he was studying medicine at Edinburgh University. Nevertheless, Bernie had soon found comfort in intimate liaisons with several women, the most regular being with his buxom neighbour Mrs Newlands whose husband was a commercial traveller and spent four nights a week away from home.

However, this did not prevent him lusting after the shapely, twenty-three-year-old Sandie and today, Bernie decided he must ask whether she was deliberately setting out to flaunt her luscious body in front of him. He loved to look at Sandie in her sexy summer clothes, particulary since she had recently remarked that she preferred dating older men 'who knew how to treat a girl properly'.

'Morning, Sandie, I've already opened the post and gone through most of the papers,' said Bernie, flashing a smile to the leggy girl. 'Would you like to pop the kettle on and then run through *The Times* and the *Guardian*? I'm knocking out a piece about our glorious South Coast climate for the P.A. tapes – I'm sure they'll use it and the Northern papers will pick it up.'

'Hope so,' she said absently and Bernie's eyes followed her as she sauntered across the room and bent down to pick up the electric kettle which was kept on the floor in the far corner of the room. He bit his lip as he watched her pull out the electric plug from the kettle. Sandie never bent her knees when she did this and it did not appear to bother her that every time she bent down, her short skirt rode up and exposed the rounded globes of her bottom which in summer were always bare, except for a tiny pair of white bikini panties.

The curvy-bodied girl straightened herself up and as she was walking out of the office to fill the kettle from the tap in the ladies cloakroom, she turned to her boss and said: 'Bernie, it's my best friend Trisha's birthday today and she's asked me out for lunch as she's taking the day off, and her boyfriend's taking her over to Brighton tonight to see the Mike and Bernie Winters show, so this'll be the only time we'll be able to get together for a chat. So, please may I have an extra half hour off at lunchtime? I'd be ever so grateful.'

'No problem, Sandie, you go and enjoy a nice long lunch with your friend,' replied Bernie generously. 'But I know how much you like Mike and Bernie Winters, so why don't you get your boyfriend, what's-his-name, Jeremy, to take you to their show? Or couldn't he get any tickets? I might be able to help you there. Johnny

Levy, the director of the Grand Theatre, owes me a favour.'

To his distress, his question caused Sandie's cheeks to colour a deep shade of red and there was a distinct quiver in her voice as she answered: 'Don't talk to me about Jeremy Greenland. He's a no good shit and I never want to see him again.'

'My, that sounds a bit ominous,' said Bernie sympathetically. 'I'm awfully sorry I mentioned him, love, but I thought you two were an item.'

'So did I,' she said with a trace of bitterness, 'but it's all over now between us after what happened last night.'

'Oh dear, is it that bad? Tell you what, make us both a nice cup of tea and if you want to get it off your chest, tell me all about it. Perhaps it's just a lovers' tiff which can be sorted out with a bit of give and take.'

'No, I told you I never want to see him again,' she snapped at him. 'I'll tell you why I've booted him out after I've made the tea because I'd like some advice, not on how to get Jeremy back, but how best I can put one over on the two-timing bastard.'

Bernie blanched at her tone for, generally speaking, Sandie had always been a sweet-tempered girl with whom he could often share a good laugh, even when life in the office became hectic. This Jeremy Greenland must really have done something pretty bad to make her react so strongly, he reflected, as he went back to typing his press release.

When he'd finished, he picked up the telephone and dialled the number of the Press Association to dictate his copy down the line. As he completed his call, Sandie returned with two mugs of tea. He sat her down on the couch and, proferring a chocolate biscuit, he said: 'Go on, love, tell Uncle Bernie all about it. I'd like to help sort this out as I don't like to see members of my crew unhappy.

You can speak freely – nothing you say will ever be given in evidence against you!'

His friendly tone dispelled Sandy's anger and she gave a small chuckle as she took a biscuit from the plate. 'Why not, it'll be interesting to see if you take my side or whether you try to excuse Jeremy on the old business of we-men-must-stick-together.'

'Now, now, you're far too young to be so cynical,' he commented with a wry smile. 'Fire away and I'll give you an honest opinion on the matter.'

Sandie munched her biscuit and then, with a heavy sigh, she told him why she had given Jeremy Greenland the order of the boot. 'It's all very simple, Bernie. For heaven's sake, you see this kind of situation happening in the films or in a book almost every day.

'I'd wanted Jeremy to take me to see *Goldfinger*, that James Bond film at the Odeon, but he phoned yesterday afternoon and said he couldn't make it because he'd forgotten that he had to play in some competition or other at his squash club. "Sorry about that," he said, and I'm not one of those girls who stamp their feet and create a big scene if their blokes let them down.

'So I said: "Never mind, it doesn't matter too much, I'll go with Dawn and Lauren instead, they're not doing anything tonight." '

Sandie stopped, pursing her lips in anger, and Bernie looked up and asked: 'And did you go with them and see *Goldfinger*?'

She nodded grimly and said: 'Sure, Trish booked the tickets and we all enjoyed the film. Afterwards we went over the road for a coffee and as Dad had let me have the car, I dropped the girls back home. It was past eleven o'clock but they live very near Jeremy's bungalow so I thought I would go round and see if he had returned home from the squash club. It looked as if he had, because his car was parked in the driveway and I could see that there was a dim light shining through the net curtains in the front room.

'So I opened his front gate and as I was walking towards the front door I heard a peculiar groaning sound that, at first, I thought was coming from round the side of the bungalow. Perhaps Minnie, Jeremy's cat, is having a night on the tiles, I said to myself, and just before I rang the doorbell I peeked through the window of the front room to see if Jeremy had actually come back because he sometimes leaves a light on to fool would-be burglars.

'Anyhow, that's when I found out that it wasn't Minnie who had been out on the tiles! The groans had been coming from my boyfriend who had been moaning with passion and, really, it was hardly surprising. There was Jeremy, before my very eyes, sprawled out on a chair with his shorts and pants round his ankles, and between his legs was kneeling a bare-breasted girl slurping her tongue up and down his cock!'

She paused for a moment and Bernie, who had been listening spell-bound to her story, tsked-tsked quietly as Sandie gulped down a draught of tea before she continued: 'I recognised the slut as Jessica Kendal, a pretty girl who was engaged to the secretary of the squash club, but although I had heard one or two rumours about her, I could still hardly believe that Jeremy could cheat on me like this. It was his idea that we should have an understanding that neither of us would play around whilst we were involved with each other.

'Honestly, I'd seen enough but I was so shocked that I just stood there and went on watching whilst Jessica finished sucking him off. Jeremy was moaning in ecstasy as she slowly lapped her way all around his knob. Then she licked her lips and plunged her head down, taking his shaft into her mouth, sucking hard and then coming up for air.

'I'll grant you that Jessica knew how to give a good gobble – she bobbed her head up and down, building up and then quelling the pressure until Jeremy gave a hoarse shout and shot his load inside her mouth. She squeezed his balls as she swallowed his spunk and I now moved away from the window and leaned back against the wall, wondering whether to ring the bell and interrupt them or just slink away and let them get on with it.'

Sandie gave a little half-smile and said: 'Well now, boss, I hope that you will agree with what I decided to do about this situation.'

Bernie frowned and took his time before replying to her. 'Whatever you did would be right, as far as I'm concerned, my dear, short of bursting in with a pair of scissors and circumcising Jeremy on the spot!'

His answer broke the tension and now Sandie smiled broadly. 'Something like that had crossed my mind,' she admitted as she finished drinking her tea, 'but in the end I simply walked back quietly to my car and drove off, leaving them to continue with their fun and games.'

'Definitely the most dignified response,' said Bernie immediately. 'And I would guess that first thing in the morning you called him up and gave him what-for over the phone – which, I may say, he most thoroughly deserved. Let's face it, when all's said and done, there isn't a red-blooded man in Falmington who wouldn't love a blow job from an attractive girl like Jessica Kendal, but it's not on if you're spoken for, and there's a world of difference between being greedy as opposed to needy!'

She nodded her agreement and said: 'Quite right, Bernie, and that's why I didn't shout or scream, but I made it plain in no uncertain terms that he was a rotten cheat who I never wanted to see again.'

'So did Jeremy try to come up with any excuse for his behaviour?'

'What excuse could he make?' she answered, shrugging her shoulders. 'He was literally caught with his trousers down and there was very little he could say except that he was very sorry and that it was only a one-off which would never happen again. But what upset me was that when I said it too late for apologies, Jeremy tried to make me feel I was at least partially to blame because I had never given him a gobble.'

Bernie's eyebrows shot up in surprise, for he would have staked folding money on Sandie being experienced in sexual play. Trying to keep his tone of voice as light as possible, he said mildly: 'Have you never tried oral sex, Sandie? I don't hold with Jeremy's argument for a moment, but I must say that if you haven't, you're missing out on something very nice indeed.'

Sandie blushed but she was not affronted by his observation. 'Perhaps I am, but the only time I've tried it, it didn't work out for me. It was a few years back just after I'd left school and started my first job. The boy's name was Mark, we were both only seventeen and he was almost as naive as me! I doubt if any girl had ever sucked his prick before because he may well have been a virgin, although I'd already lost my cherry after drinking too much at Trish's seventeenth birthday party. So neither of us were what you'd call sexually experienced.

'Anyway, we hadn't done more than to snog on the sofa late at night when my parents were asleep, and we almost went all the way one night. I'd let Mark pull down my panties and finger my pussy whilst I had unzipped his flies and was playing with his prick.

'Then he started to push my head down to his lap, and I knew that he wanted me to suck his cock. Truthfully, I was a bit scared but I thought I would have a go, so I held his shaft steady in my hand and leaned forward and planted a big wet kiss on the top of his helmet. "Oh, that's super," he gasped. "Please do that again."

'So I did and I admit I quite liked doing it, but this time he thrust his knob into my mouth and I nearly choked on it. In fact, I did gag on his shaft and I quickly moved my head up, spluttering for air, and that was that. I've never tried sucking a prick again, although I've had a couple of boyfriends who've brought me off beautifully with their mouths and, incidentally, that's more than Jeremy ever did!'

'Well, I'm sure you're not the first girl ever to be put off oral sex by an inconsiderate or too eager lover,' mused Bernie, whose own shaft had been stirring uncomfortably in his trousers during Sandie's frank confession. 'Such a shame, though, because not only me but many other people would say that oral sex can give the greatest sensations of all.'

'Yes, I've heard that from other boys and one or two girls, too,' she agreed thoughtfully, and then suddenly she perked up and lifted her head. 'Hey, that reminds me of a joke Trish told me yesterday. Do you know the difference between an egg and a blow job? No? Well, you can beat an egg!'

Bernie laughed out loud and blew her a reassuring kiss across the table. 'One day you'll find that out for yourself. You're bound to meet up with a more skilled and experienced partner with whom you will want to have another try. And I jolly well hope you do, because I'm sure the only barrier stopping you enjoying oral sex is in your mind, and once that barrier is breached you'll love it as much as I do.'

Sandie gave him a cheeky look. 'Perhaps that's why I prefer older men. You know, I might be subconsciously looking for someone to guide me and all that sort of jazz.'

But before Bernie could respond, there was a sharp knock on the door and Councillor Goulthorp came into the office. 'Morning all,' he said briskly. 'Well, Mr Gosling, this lovely weather is just what the doctor ordered, and I certainly hope you've got some ideas to make the most of it.'

Here comes trouble, groaned Bernie, for the councillor was a former business tycoon from Garforth, who had lived with his wife in Falmington since he had accepted early retirement and a substantial tax-free golden handshake from the large public company which had taken over his Leeds-based canned foods business in 1963. A genuine music lover, he had generously provided several new instruments for the town's brass band of which he was the deputy conductor, but he had not properly prepared for retirement and was finding life somewhat irksome.

Then, more because of subtle pressure from his wife who wanted him out of the house during the day than any genuine political convictions, he stood as an Independent in a council by-election in late 1963. Perhaps because he was able to spend more time and money canvassing a very indifferent electorate than either the Labour, Liberal or Conservative candidates, to his great delight he scraped home by four votes, though he subsequently won again by a three-figure margin in the full Council election held eighteen months later when the Conservatives' majority fell to only two and all three parties made off-the-record overtures that they would support his nomination to be Mayor of Falmington next year if he would cast his vote with their group at Council meetings.

Mr Goulthorp replied to them all that he would consider his position and to be fair, he deserved the honour for he had worked like a Trojan on the Council, putting in endless hours in various committees. So much so that Mrs Goulthorp began to regret her original idea and begged him to give up his seat at the next election.

Meanwhile, he was convinced that the municipal employees should be far more careful with ratepayers' money, and Bernie Gosling dreaded the councillor's visits to his office, especially if he was carrying a photostat of the publicity department's expenses, because that would mean a rigorous cross-examination on, for instance, why Bernie thought it necessary to have a beer and sandwiches lunch with Cyril Stanmore, the editor of the *Falmington Telegraph* at The Three Tuns almost every week.

However, to Bernie's relief, Mr Goulthorp was in his office not to check up on flagrant misuse of Council funds, but rather to know whether the leaflets advertising the town band's open-air concert the following afternoon had arrived back from the printers.

'Not till tomorrow morning, I'm afraid, but they always said it would be difficult to promise delivery before Wednesday,' said Bernie, and the councillor clicked his teeth in irritation.

'By the heck, they don't hurry themselves,' he observed tartly. 'Well, I'll make sure that when their bill comes in we'll take our time paying it. More important, though, I want to see lots of bums on seats for this concert and not just because I'm conducting the second half. It's because, in case you hadn't heard, Councillor McGill wants us to withdraw our financial support for the town band because she thinks that our kind of music is behind the times.'

He put on a high falsetto voice and mimicked the 'loony left' Miss McGill: 'Young people don't want to hear that jingoistic military rubbish these days, we should be encouraging local pop groups to give free performances at the bandstand like the Rolling Stones in Hyde Park.'

'Well, I don't think that's such a terrible idea,' said Sandie, nonchalantly uncrossing her bare legs as she brushed some biscuit crumbs from her skirt, an action which temporarily discomfited their visitor. 'I mean, I don't hold with scrapping the band, because lots of people like listening to it, especially if the weather's good. But I don't see why we shouldn't put on a rock 'n' roll show one afternoon and give local kids their chance to show what they can do.'

Bernie could not prevent a little chuckle escaping from his throat. 'Well, that sounds like a good idea to me. If you could organise it perhaps in conjunction with the youth clubs it would cost very little to stage and we'd have another attraction for younger holidaymakers, and we'd show a profit into the bargain. What do you say, Councillor?'

Mr Goulthorp looked at him with undisguised horror. 'No, no, it wouldn't do at all,' he said, shaking his head testily. 'I'm not such an old stick-in-the-mud as you very well know, young lady, and I'll say here and now, despite their dreadful hairstyles, that Lennon and McCartney in particular are two very talented lads and I've no time at all for those foolish folk who sent back their medals to the Queen as a protest because the Beatles were given the M.B.E.

'But what kind of audience would such a show attract? I grant you might get new people coming into Falmington, but do we want a crowd of drug-taking hippies and girls dancing topless on our seafront, let alone hordes of those Mods and Rockers clogging up the roads and causing all kinds of mayhem?'

You wouldn't mind the topless girls, thought Bernie as he said: 'I don't think we'd have these problems if the project was properly organised. Anyhow, we've enough on our plate for now, though you might like to think about the idea for next year. Meanwhile, as soon as the leaflets come in for the brass band concert, I'll send copies over to your office.'

'Bernie, you disappoint me,' said Sandie as she rose to her feet, a sulky expression on her face which made her lips pout prettily outwards as she marched towards the door with the two empty mugs in her hand. 'If you really think a pop concert is a good idea, why not put one on later this month? You said yourself it wouldn't be difficult to manage and wouldn't cost anything but time, so I don't see why you need to dither about making a decision. Strike whilst the iron is hot, that's what you've always believed, isn't it, Mr Goulthorp?'

With that tirade, Sandie stalked across the room leaving Bernie and Mr Goulthorp staring at the rounded cheeks of her tight little backside which salaciously wiggled from side to side as she walked out of the office to deposit the mugs in the kitchen.

'I suppose she has a point,' sighed Bernie, thinking that the councillor would tell him to forget such nonsense and make even more strenuous efforts to cut his department's expenses. But to his surprise, Mr Goulthorp did not dismiss the idea out of hand. Instead, he ran his finger along the inside of his collar and scowled briefly before replying: 'She has indeed and perhaps you should consider the idea very carefully. I can't say the thought of holding a pop music concert fills me with joy. It's not just the music which isn't my scene but the rowdiness which goes with it which worries me.

'Young people today are very different to what they were like in my time. For a start, good manners have gone right out of the window. When I was a lad you offered your seat to a lady in a train or a bus, but that kind of politeness seems to have vanished without trace. As I was saying to Councillor Fletcher in the bar last night, any behaviour short of farting at a funeral appears to be acceptable these days.'

Bernie was curious to know the reason for this sudden

change of tack but for the present he said mildly: 'Come on, that's a bit of a harsh generalisation. Schoolboys might not doff their caps to their elders and betters any more, but I've seen lots of courtesy shown by teenagers right here in Falmington. For starters, look how many kids from the Youth Club volunteered to help out with Meals On Wheels for the old folk during their school holidays?'

Mr Goulthorp stroked his chin as he mulled this over and finally concluded: 'Aye lad, mebbe you're right at that. Well, you set out a paper for me about why we should put on a pop concert, with full details of what costs would be involved, and send it to me. As deputy chairman of the Leisure Committee, I'll be able to give you a quick yea or nay.'

He consulted his watch and added: 'I must be getting on and I'm sure you have plenty of work to do. Send me that report as soon as possible, though, and if I were you I would involve Miss Walters, she obviously knows what would appeal to the younger age groups.'

Stranger and stranger, muttered Bernie quietly as Mr Goulthorp closed the office door behind him, for the councillor was hardly the progressive kind of chap who agreed with all these fashionable feminist theories which had been so widely discussed in the papers and on television for the last couple of years. Indeed, he would have wagered his salary on Goulthorp being 'a woman's place is in the home, especially the kitchen and bedroom' sort of saloon bar type.

'Perhaps you can explain why old Goulthorp now wants me to prepare a paper on putting on your blinking pop concert,' he said to Sandie as she returned to her desk.

She gave an enigmatic shrug and said: 'Well, you'd best ask him yourself, I'm sure he'll tell you the reason why he changed his mind.'

It was apparent from her answer and the secret little

smile on her face as she sat down to finish poring through the *Guardian* for any story which might be of interest to Bernie, that Sandie knew more than she was letting on. So Bernie decided he would hold his tongue and say nothing more until he had prepared the report, by which time Sandie might hopefully let him into the secret. With this in mind, Bernie began making his preliminary notes on the proposed pop music concert and pondered the question as to whether his sexy assistant had anything to do with Councillor Goulthorp's sudden conversion to backing the idea.

At roughly the same time as Bernie was taxing his brain over this further task which had landed on his plate, slightly over a mile away in the imposing headquarters of Falmington College of Higher Education, set in its own grounds in the smart residential area bounded by Randall Road and Suffield Avenue, Grahame Johnstone and Philippa Farthing, his fresh-faced young secretary, were engaged in a more down-to-earth activity.

After she had locked the door, Philippa had slipped off her knickers and standing with her feet slightly apart, had leaned forward and sprawled her nubile body over the conference table, resting her cheek on the polished maple surface.

Grahame Johnstone, who was the newly appointed senior lecturer in French and German, looked up from the pile of papers on his desk and gave an approving little growl of approval. But to Philippa's annoyance, he did not immediately shoot out of his chair and rip down his trousers.

'Well, if you don't want to fuck me—' she started to complain but Grahame held up his hand and stopped her in mid-sentence. 'Hold on a moment, I must just finish marking this piece by Suzie Brush, and then I'll be with you,' he explained, scanning through the final paragraph of the essay as he rose to his feet.

'Huh! I sometimes wonder if you've ever offered her an extra couple of marks to let you feel her tits!' she said scornfully. 'Come on, Grahame, I want you to put that paper down and stick your big cock in my nookie – but you'd better hurry, the offer closes in ten seconds!'

Hastily, he scrawled a *B+* on Suzie Brush's work, and rushed across to the waiting Philippa who had begun counting down: 'Ten, nine, eight, seven, six – oooh, oooh! Carry on, Grahame, I adore the way you smooth your hands across my bottom, it really turns me on.'

'Good show,' muttered the lecturer as he lifted her short skirt to reveal her bare backside, and Philippa heard her lover slide to his knees and she let out a tiny squeal as first Grahame kissed and then clutched each of her dimpled buttocks in his hands. The soft flesh of her beautiful bum cheeks so close to his face inevitably made him tremble with desire and as he parted the rounded globes he licked his lips at the sight of the pink, pouting lips of her quim.

Without further delay he forced his head between her thighs and slid the tip of his tongue inside her moistening cunny and, to his gratification, the slender nineteen-year-old girl squealed again with delight as the curled point of his tongue found the edges of her clitty and his hands snaked upwards and round her back to cup her small but firmly rounded breasts, whilst his tongue now slipped in and out of her cunt with ease, coated with the love juice which had started to trickle out of her honeypot.

When he judged that her pussy was ready for his cock, Grahame scrambled to his feet and Phillipa turned her head and watched him tear down his trousers and pants, waiting eagerly to see his massive stiff shaft which would shortly be sliding its way inside her juicy love channel.

Size might not matter, she had told Carole, her best friend who worked for Dr Radleigh, the principal of the college, but no-one could persuade her that a prick like Grahame Johnstone's that measured over nine and a half inches wasn't worth its weight in gold.

'Okay, here we go!' cried Grahame as he moved behind her, nudging her knees slightly further apart as he took his throbbing tool in his hand and slowly guided the gleaming purplish helmet into the soft folds of her pussy from behind. Once he was fully inside her he began to fuck her with sharp, jabbing strokes, with his hands back on her breasts whilst Philippa caught his rhythm and jerked her hips to and fro in perfect time with his quick, short shoves in and out of her juicy cunny.

Philippa's body pulsated with pleasure and she urged him on as Grahame now changed the pace and style of the fuck, driving the powerful length of his rigid rod fully inside her. He rode his prick in and out of her clinging crack until his cock triggered Philippa's cunt into the ultimate ecstasy – and as she yelped with joy as the force of her climax rocketed through her body, Grahame grunted heavily as his cock shot out a fierce fountain of sticky white spunk inside her tingling cunny.

He withdrew his deflated shaft from between her bum cheeks but Philippa was a feisty girl who was not satisfied with one short bout of lovemaking. 'Come on, Grahame, don't stop now,' she demanded as she turned round to see her lover mopping his brow. 'Take a couple of cushions from that armchair behind you and we can have a nice comfortable fuck on the floor.'

'I'd love to, Phil, but I doubt if I'll be able to get another hard-on for a while,' said Grahame sadly, remembering with a sigh how he could wank through the night when he was fifteen and devoutly wishing that he was in his mid-teens again, although he comforted himself with the knowledge that at twenty-eight he was a better, more sophisticated lover than any of the teenage studs with whom the lusty seventeen-year-old Philippa consorted late on Saturday nights.

'Never mind, I'm crazy about the way you bring me off with your tongue,' she replied perkily, sliding her hand up and down Grahame's limp shaft to make sure there was no chance of coaxing it back into life.

'Okay then,' he agreed, tossing Phillipa the two cushions which she caught as she lay down on the light green carpet. She lay on her back, resting her head on one and sliding the other underneath her bottom. Then Grahame placed himself between her parted thighs and without further ado she pulled his head down to her fluffy brown bush and he kissed her pouting pussy lips which made her gasp with excitement.

Then he lifted his left arm and let his hand travel over her body until he found her breasts, and he tweaked her stubby red nipples, first one and then the other, whilst his other hand pressed firmly upon her hairy mound. 'Aaah, that's the way,' she encouraged him as his fingers glided along the length of her sopping slit, and Philippa purred with delight when he inserted two fingers inside her juicy gash and began to slide them in and out at an ever-increasing pace.

Her lithe body began to writhe under this remorseless frigging and when her erect little clitty popped out of its sheath, Grahame sucked it between his lips and Philippa came almost at once, sending a spurt of tangy cuntal juice into his mouth. Grahame gulped it down and continued to suck even harder, pushing his mouth up against her cunt, moving his head back and forth as his tongue swirled along the silken grooves of her love channel, licking and lapping the juices which were now pumping out of her pussy.

With each stroke Philippa arched her body in ecstasy, pressing her twitching clitty up against the tip of his flickering tongue as her cunny exploded again and Grahame's face was spattered with a fresh outpouring of pussy juice.

'OOOOH!' she screamed out so loudly that Grahame pulled his face away from her dripping muff and whispered a warning to the excited girl to calm herself down.

He placed a finger to his lips and muttered: 'Sssh, Philly, for heaven's sake don't make such a noise, all we need is for Dr Radleigh to come knocking at the door and we'll both be out of a job.'

'Sorry, darling' she apologised as she gulped in and exhaled a series of deep breaths of air whilst she recovered from her climax, and then added reproachfully: 'But you're the one who's to blame, Grahame Johnstone, licking out my pussy so beautifully. No boy has ever managed to bring me off with his tongue like you can. You make me feel so randy, you old sexpot, that I only have to look at you for my panties to get damp!'

Naturally, this tribute to his sexual prowess pleased him, but Grahame was still concerned about being caught *in flagrante delicto* with the young teenager. 'Thanks for the compliment, love. Believe me, I'd much rather make love to you than mark all these damned essays, but we must take care not to broadcast the fact that we've been fucking instead of working! God, can you just imagine what Dr Radleigh would say if he knew what we've been up to?'

'He'd be absolutely livid – and bloody jealous too, I've seen him trying to flash a look up my skirt when I've been in the library, standing on a stepladder getting out some books for you,' Philippa giggled and Grahame nodded fervently. 'Well, there you go then. All the more reason for us to be discreet when we make love at the College.'

Normally, Grahame would have been justified in impressing upon his partner the need to take sensible precautions against discovery. However, whilst he had been fucking Philippa, Dr Edwin Radleigh, the Principal of Falmington College of Higher Education, had been far too busy trying to hide a bulging erection in his trousers from a most attractive new member of the summer school staff who was sitting a few feet away from him in his study, showing a generous measure of shapely thigh as she crossed her legs without pulling down her short tight skirt.

Miss Rosie O'Hara was a most attractive young woman in her late twenties, blessed not only with a pretty oval face with large dark eyes, but with wide lips made even more eye-catching by a liberal application of bright red lipstick and full, rounded breasts which swelled seductively under her creamy silk blouse.

In fact, this was the first time Dr Radleigh had made Miss O'Hara's acquaintance, for she had been engaged by his deputy whilst he had been on vacation with his wife, the fearsome and feared headmistress of Falmington Secondary School. Rosie O'Hara was a sociologist and Dr Radleigh, himself a mathematician, had an instinctive distrust of anything and anybody concerned with such an inexact science, and one which seemed to present problems without offering any solutions.

However, he realised that he needed a noted guest lecturer in sociology for the summer school curriculum and was very pleasantly surprised when his secretary ushered Rosie O'Hara into his study for a short meeting before her first seminar. Whilst engaging in smalltalk while Miss Satterthwaite prepared coffee, they discovered that Dr Radleigh's Irish grandmother hailed from the same area of Wicklow as the O'Hara family and soon they were chatting cosily away like old friends.

Edwin Radleigh was instantly attracted to the sensual

sociologist, and to his slight embarassment, for luckily he was sitting behind his desk, his penis uncoiled and thrust itself up into a state of throbbing erection as Rosie began to talk about what she planned to say about sexuality to her students in her first lecture on the coming Friday.

'I was educated in a small country school in Ireland,' she explained, as she uncrossed her legs, and Dr Radleigh inhaled sharply when she smoothed her hand down her skirt and let it rest on her shapely knee for a few moments before picking up her cup and saucer. 'And you couldn't have a better example than how the Church and State still teach children that their own bodies are sinful. Honestly, Dr Radleigh—'

'Edwin, please, don't let's stand on ceremony – we will be working closely together over the next few weeks,' he interjected, and Rosie flashed him a winning smile as she gave a little gracious nod.

'Fine, well as I was saying, Edwin, it was no wonder that the kids at my school grew up convinced that all sexual expression was wrong and they themselves were going to hell on a broomstick if they gave in to the most basic, natural biological drives. Father Block used to terrify the boys by warning them that they would go blind if they masturbated, and the nuns were forever warning the girls not to touch their private parts.

'This created a deep-seated guilt in the minds of the youngsters and I'm sure that this affects many Irish men and women in adult life. Luckily, some more enlightened church leaders are abandoning their traditional attempt to stifle sexual awareness amongst ordinary people.'

Dr Radleigh cleared his throat and commented: 'Yes, well I suppose this is hardly surprising. I'm sure that throughout history many freedoms have been denied individuals and groups because those in power have feared that if certain restraints were lifted, this would lead to an undermining of the established authority.'

'Edwin, I can't tell you how pleased I am that we are of the same mind about this matter. My last principal was such a dyed-in-the-wool traditionalist that we fought like cat and dog every day,' said Rosie, her dark eyes shining with pleasure. 'And so you'll agree that until recently it was very difficult for an ill-informed public to make a reasoned analysis as to whether this established authority was in fact beneficial to the society concerned, whilst any changes were resisted by those in power because change itself was considered highly dangerous to the social order.

'However, we're living in a time when at last the ruling élite can no longer control the superstitious uneducated masses. In the realm of sexuality, for example, men and women will soon no longer be ashamed of their so-called dirty parts and will be able to enjoy the delights of copulation without feeling bad about it!' she concluded triumphantly as, after giving a short knock on the door, Miss Satterthwaite opened it to remind Dr Radleigh that Mr Teplin, the noted professor of business administration and management from the London School of Economics, who was the most important guest lecturer in the summer school programme, had already been waiting for five minutes to see him.

Dr Radleigh frowned as he looked at his watch, for he did not want to give offence to his star tutor. 'Oh yes, I had asked him to come and see at half past eleven. Please tell him I'll be with him directly,' he replied, but when Miss Satterthwaite closed the door behind her, he turned back to Rosie O'Hara and said: 'Rosie, I wonder if we could continue this fascinating discussion over lunch. There's a nice little pub I know on the Brighton Road which serves very decent meals. It'll only take fifteen minutes at the most to get there in the car.'

'Thank you very much, Edwin, that would be very

nice,' answered Rosie, and the principal beamed with satisfaction as, forgetting about the protrusion which was still noticeable in the front of his trousers, he stood up and leaned across his desk to shake hands with her.

'Splendid, shall we meet at the front entrance at a quarter to one?' he suggested as he escorted her to the door to his secretary's outer office.

Rosie looked briefly at the bulge between Edwin Radleigh's legs. 'Fine, I look forward to seeing you later,' she promised, leaving Dr Radleigh with a cheery smile on his face as Miss Satterthwaite went to fetch the waiting Mr Teplin who had wandered into the corridor to study the notice-board.

'Sorry to have kept you waiting, Bruce,' said Dr Radleigh when the professor ambled back with Miss Satterthwaite. 'Do sit down. Now, what can I do for you? No problems with our students, I hope.'

Bruce Teplin shook his head. 'None at all, by and large they're one of the most hard-working, intelligent groups I've worked with for some time. But I do have a problem about which I would value your advice.'

He paused for a moment and then continued: 'Edwin, may I speak to you in complete confidence?'

'Of course you may, Bruce,' Dr Radleigh reassured him, and to do justice to the principal, he had been given no reason to know that for some time now, whenever he entertained anyone in his study, it had been the common practice of the nosey Miss Satterthwaite to eavesdrop by keeping her ear firmly pressed to the keyhole in order to glean any interesting gossip. 'Nothing you say will go further than these four walls, so you can be totally frank in telling me what is on your mind.'

Bruce Teplin nervously ran his hand across his mouth. 'I'll say at the start that I've been very foolish,' he said with a sigh. 'But, on the other hand, it would have taken more willpower than anyone I know to have resisted horny Helen and her bosom friend, Barbie.'

'Horny Helen and her bosom friend, Barbie?' echoed a puzzled Dr Radleigh. 'I'm afraid I don't quite follow you.'

'You would have done last night given half a chance,' riposted the professor with a ghost of a smile playing about his lips. 'And in my opinion, so would ninety-nine per cent of all the heterosexual men in Falmington! Anyhow, I'd best start at the beginning. You know I'm staying at the Langham Park Hotel, your office made all the arrangements before I arrived.'

'Yes, of course, I made the booking myself,' said Dr Radleigh. 'Dear, Oh dear, I'm surprised you have a complaint to make about it, the Langham Park is one of the best hotels along this stretch of the coast. The proprietor, Mr Amos, is a personal friend and he'll be terribly upset to hear if anything at the hotel is not to your liking.'

'The hotel itself is fine,' Mr Teplin acknowledged as he rubbed his nose. 'The rooms are clean and very comfortable whilst the food is very good. No, my problem is, um, a rather personal matter which concerns me and two of the hotel's chambermaids.'

'Ah, I see,' said Dr Radleigh. 'In that case, perhaps it would be best that I don't telephone Mr Amos,' and there was a brief silence during which Miss Satterthwaite took the receiver off her telephone to ensure there would be no interruptions before cementing her ear back firmly to the keyhole.

Bruce Teplin agreed: 'Yes, it would be best indeed not to involve him. However, I must tell you about something which happened two days ago. I'd been stuck inside the college all afternoon and the weather was so warm when I left the college that I thought I'd make the most of the sunshine and walk back to the Langham Park instead of ordering my usual taxi. But I hadn't realised just how hot it was and by the time I got back to the hotel, I was dripping with perspiration and as I pushed open the swing door I decided I would go straight up to my room and take a shower before dinner.

'But when I asked for my room key at the reception desk, Mr Ridout, the duty manager, bustled up and said to me: "Mr Teplin, I'm terribly sorry but we've had a problem with one of the pipes leading to your bathroom and there's no hot water. The plumber is working on it right now but he doesn't expect to be finished for another couple of hours. So may I give you the key to number twenty-seven which is just two doors away from your room? It's empty till tomorrow afternoon so you can use the bathroom until the plumber has finished."

'This was no great inconvenience, so I took the key to the spare room from him and went upstairs to my own room and undressed. I put on my dressing gown and slippers and walked down to number twenty-seven. I had been told that the room was empty but I could have sworn that I could hear the sound of giggling coming from inside the room.

'The noise must be coming from the next room, I thought to myself as I turned the key in the door and walked in – only to find that I was far from imagining anything of the sort! Lying together stark naked on the double bed were the two good-looking young chamber-maids who had been introduced to me when I first arrived at the hotel. I remembered the blonde girl, who was flat on her back with her eyes closed and a smile of satisfaction on her face, had told me that her name was Helen, but I couldn't recall the name of the other girl, who was busy kissing Helen's titties whilst she was rubbing her hand across her silky golden muff.

'The girls had been so wrapped up in their love-making

that they hadn't even heard me come in. I stood there for a few seconds and then I called out: "Hey! What are you two doing in here?"

'Helen opened her eyes and sat bolt upright. "Mr Teplin! What are *you* doing in here? You're in number twenty-three and no-one is due in this room till tomorrow afternoon."

' "Yes, that's quite right, but as there's no hot water in my room, Mr Ridout gave me the key to this one," I said somewhat sternly. But her friend, whose name I suddenly remembered was Barbie, tossed her head and said grudgingly: "Well I suppose you would like us to leave, but really, old Ridout might have told us that you were going to use this room."

' "Oh, I don't see why you need to be disturbed," I said, hardly able to take my eyes off the luscious red chink between Helen's pouting pussy lips which appeared when she moved her legs slightly apart. Helen saw the direction of my gaze and, turning to her friend, said in a husky voice: "Barbie, I don't think we'll have to go. Unless I'm very wrong, Mr Teplin would like to stay and watch us. Would you mind very much if he did?"

' "No, not if you don't," replied Barbie with a wicked glint in her eye, and she looked me up and down and said: "You might as well take a seat, sir, there's no extra charge for watching the show."

'So I plonked myself down on a chair and the girls started playing with each other as if I were back in my own room. Barbie tweaked up Helen's nipples till they were sticking out like two rubbery nuggets as the blonde girl grasped Barbie's chubby bum cheeks and fondled them, whilst she pushed her big titties up in front of Barbie's lips and the girl sucked and licked on the ripe red cherries as she parted her thighs to receive Barbie's hand on her neatly trimmed, corn-coloured mound of pussy hair.

'Barbie slowly ran a finger along the long crack of Helen's cunny and when Barbie slid a finger up to the top knuckle inside her squelchy cunt, Helen whimpered with pleasure. Then she slid a second finger into Helen's honeypot and athletically leaped on top of her partner, and straddled her so that her rounded rump was poised directly over Helen's mouth. She gently lowered her backside and Helen took hold of her bum cheeks and I peered forward to see Helen insert her tongue between them into the quivering folds of her pussy. Barbie leaned forward and dived into Helen's silky wet thatch to complete a perfect "sixty-nine" as they licked out each other's cunts, probing, sucking and rubbing, frigging themselves up to a frenzy and shrieking with joy as they shuddered up to a glorious mutual climax.'

'My God! I would have been beside myself by now!' exclaimed Dr Radleigh, and Bruce Teplin let out a hoarse chuckle as he nodded and said: 'That's precisely what I was, Edwin! I could hardly contain myself as the girls continued to play with each other, grinding their pussies together, and then Helen rolled on top of Barbie and rubbed herself suggestively against her, wiggling her bottom at me.

'Naturally my prick was now stiff as a poker and bursting to get in on the action, so when Helen turned her head round and called out: "Come on, Brucie, wouldn't your cock like to be the meat in the sandwich?" she didn't have to ask twice! I tore off my dressing gown and climbed onto the bed where Barbie took hold of my shaft in her hand and said: "Now I know what my friend likes, Bruce. She wants you to fuck her bum. You don't have any objection, have you?"

' "None whatsoever," I stuttered, and when she took my tool between her lips and started to suck noisily on my knob, Helen giggled and called out: 'Don't forget what we were taught at school, Barbie, chew every mouthful thoroughly before swallowing!'

'I pressed her head down as Barbie's mouth closed over my helmet and she sucked in my cock to the very root, cupping my balls in her hand. But then Helen swung herself round and leaned on her elbows and knees, raising her gorgeous bottom high in the air. Then, cradling her head on her arm and looking backwards at me through the gap between her parted thighs, she cooed to Barbie: "Don't be a spoilsport and milk his prick before he's fucked me. You can always suck him off afterwards."

'Reluctantly, Barbie opened her mouth and released my trembling tool with a farewell kiss as I placed my hands on the fleshy buttocks of Helen's lovely arse. And you can take my word for it, Edwin, this girl really has a beautiful backside with soft peachy cheeks and a delicious cleft between them. When I pulled them apart I saw the inviting little bum-hole winking at me below the sopping hair of her pussy and Barbie muttered: "Carry on, Bruce, you can go through the tradesmen's entrance. Helen loves to be bum-fucked once in a while, don't you, you naughty girl?"

' "Oh yes, and I'm just in the mood for it too," gasped Helen whilst Barbie prepared my cock by licking my shaft, wetting it further with saliva and carefully placing the tip of my knob at the entrance to Helen's wrinkled rear dimple. I pushed forward slowly and she squirmed and twisted around so much that although I continued to piston my prick inside her until my balls were brushing against her backside, I anxiously asked Helen whether I should perhaps withdraw an inch or two of my shaft from her back passage.

' "No, no, just push further in and let me feel your fat cock inside me," she whispered, and sure enough her bottom responded to every shove as I pushed home, feeling her sphincter muscle release and the walls of her back passage widen as I pumped away. I put my left hand round her shoulders and began rubbing her nipples whilst my right hand went under her thigh and I stuck two stiff fingers inside her juicy honeypot, holding them still because the jerking of her hips whilst I fucked her bum enabled Helen to frig herself on my fingers at the same time.

'Helen really enjoyed being taken this way and she let out a series of loud, ecstatic groans and she must have come at least three times before I shot my load, pumping spurts of hot, creamy jism inside her bum.'

Dr Radleigh fingered the inside of his collar as he sat back in his chair and commented: 'Well, so far so good, I don't know what you're worried about. I'll wager that all the other male guests would be highly envious if they knew the girls had chosen you to be their sex toy. As a matter of interest, were you able to turn your attention to Barbie or had this unexpected encounter with Helen exhausted you?'

Despite his professed unease, Bruce Teplin grinned as he replied: 'Sure, I was dead to the world but after a while I perked up, especially when the girls began playing with each other and fingering each other's pussies. Barbie threw herself backwards and opened her legs wide as Helen dived down and placed her face between her playmate's thighs and nuzzled her lips inside Barbie's thick brown bush.

' "Ohhh! Ohhh! Ohhh! That's divine, darling – now be an angel and finish me off!" cried Barbie, clutching Helen's head whilst she pressed her mouth against her pussy.

' "I can do that for you," I offered, holding my revived, rock-hard rod in my hand. Helen scrambled to her knees and, most unselfishly I must say, took one look at my stiffie and said: "All right then, you fuck Barbie whilst I kiss your balls."

'She planted a lingering, wet kiss on my bell-end and swirled her tongue around it before taking it in her hand and guiding my knob towards Barbie's pouting pink pussy lips.

' "Brace yourself, Barbie," Helen warned as I slid three inches of stiff cock inside Barbie's squishy cunny. But she need not have worried as Barbie was easily able to accommodate my throbbing tool inside her love-box, and she whimpered with delight as I started to fuck her with long, slow strokes, pulling out my prick almost to the tip and then sliding it back home up to the root till the hairs around our pubes became entangled.

'Then Helen moved her head down to begin sucking my balls as I built up a rhythm, pushing my prick in and out of Barbie's willing, wet cunt, and her cunny muscles squeezed tightly round my shaft whilst Helen continued to lick my tightening ballsack. I drove deeper and deeper until I could no longer hold back and a gush of sticky jism gushed out of my knob into her love crack. I managed to keep my cock stiff enough to continue riding in and out of her sopping slit till I was able to trigger Barbie's cunt into a climax, and it was most gratifying to hear her wail: "I've come! I've come!" just as my shaft began to shrink back into limpness, and she threw her arms around my neck and kissed me as the three of us rolled around in ecstasy on the soft bed.'

He exhaled a deep breath and there was a long silence as Bruce Teplin savoured the memory of this erotic romp, and Edwin Radleigh thought to himself that far from having anything about which to complain, his visitor should be writing to all the tourist guides to suggest that an extra star rating should be given to the Langham Park Hotel!

'I hope you don't mind my saying so,' said Dr Radleigh eventually, trying his best to keep any note of reproach or envy out of his voice. 'But if I were in your position I would be jumping for joy. Good heavens, I've attended conferences and what have you all over the country, but I've never been fortunate enough to meet such willing girls as the chambermaids at the Langham Park.'

Bruce Tepling blushed and pursed his lips. 'I know, Edwin, and you're quite in order to say so, but the point is that on Friday my fiancée is coming to Falmington to stay with me for a long weekend. Remember that you kindly obliged me by booking a double room 'for Mr and Mrs Teplin' to save any embarrassment about having anyone but my wife sharing my room.

Behind the door of Dr Radleigh's study, Miss Satterthwaite could hardly contain herself and her whole body twitched with curiosity as she listened to Bruce Teplin continue: 'As you rightly say, I had no cause for complaint and it would have been sensible to chalk the incident up as a lucky break and walk away from the situation. But I was greedy, and when the girls suggested a further session later that night, I agreed and just before midnight, there was a knock on my door and the two girls piled in and we screwed in every conceivable way.

'I opened up the mini-bar in my room and we finished off two bottles of wine and, to be honest, I became so tired that I fell asleep whilst the girls were lying with their heads on my thighs taking turns to gobble my cock. They left before I woke up in the morning and, whilst I was dressing, I decided that as Fiona would soon be arriving at the hotel, I'd better warn the girls that I wouldn't be available for any further frolics.

'Then I remembered that I needed to show someone on the hotel staff a little gift I had bought for Fiona back in town just before I came down to Falmington. I'd been lucky enough to pick up an exquisite Edwardian ladies' perfume bottle in cut glass with hinged caps and chased silver in one of those interesting antique shops around Camden Passage in Islington, but the bottle was crying out for a good dab of Silvo and some elbow grease to get rid of the grime, and I knew that a ten bob note to the hotel housekeeper would make it sparkle like new.

'When I was ready to go down to breakfast I looked in the top drawer of the dressing table for the bottle but couldn't find it. Now I was certain I'd put it in this particular drawer because I remembered how pretty it looked when I laid it down on a white handkerchief.'

Dr Radleigh drummed his fingers on his desk. 'And you think that one of the girls has stolen the bottle?' he asked bluntly.

'I'm as good as certain of it,' came back the unhappy retort from Bruce Teplin. 'Just as I distinctly recall putting the bottle in the drawer, I also recollect telling Helen when she asked if I had a handkerchief she could use that she would find one in the top drawer of my dressing table, and she slipped out of bed to get it. I was busy playing with Barbie's breasts at the time so I didn't actually see her open the drawer, but . . .'

He left the rest of the sentence unsaid and Dr Radleigh pursed his lips and asked: 'Does your fiancée know anything about the bottle? If it's any consolation, there's much truth in the old saying that what the mind doesn't know, the heart won't grieve over.'

'True enough, Edwin, and it's just as well that Fiona wasn't with me when I bought the thing, so I've only lost the tenner I paid for it. But that's not the point, the fact is that I've been robbed by a member of the Langham Park hotel staff, but I'm damned if I know how I can report the theft without getting myself into a heap of trouble at the same time.'

'M'ph, I see your point,' said the principal with a sage nod of his head. 'Bruce, I think the best course of action is for you to leave this matter in my hands. Noel Amos, the owner of the Langham Park, is an old friend of mine and I can speak to him in strict confidence I'm sure he'll be able to solve this dilemma for your before your fiancée arrives here on Friday.'

'You really think so?' asked the troubled Professor Teplin, and Dr Radleigh replied: 'I do indeed and furthermore, knowing Noel Amos, I am equally sure you will soon have the perfume bottle in your possession in good time to present it to your fiancée.'

After his visitor had left the office in a far happier state of mind, fortuitously as unaware as Dr Radleigh of Miss Satterthwaite's eavesdropping at the keyhole. But as it was to turn out, no great damage was to be done by the secretary's listening in to the private discussion of this delicate matter.

# CHAPTER FOUR

## *Seaside Scandals*

When he had first steered his MGB into the car park of the Langham Park Hotel, Nick Armitage still had a few remaining doubts in his mind as to whether he had been sensible to take up the company's proposal that he immerse himself in a crash course in French, even though in his pocket lay a comforting letter from Dave Harrow, the financial director of Gottlieb Fashions, confirming an immediate £500 a year raise in his salary with a promise that if he passed the examination at the end of his studies at Falmington College of Higher Education and accepted the position of director of European sales, Alan Gottlieb would be pleased to double this increase to a cool extra thousand pounds a year.

However, to his own surprise, Nick found that he had remembered more rules of French grammar than he had realised from his schooldays, and he had struck up a firm friendship with Grahame Johnstone who, buoyed up by whirlwind daily fucking with his luscious teenage siren, Philippa Farthing, had soon proved himself to be a first class tutor who motivated his students through his evident enthusiasm and ability to teach with quiet effectiveness, patience and understanding.

Whilst Dr Radleigh was driving Rosie O'Hara to a *tête à tête* lunch in a small country pub on the Brighton Road,

113

back in Falmington in the bar of *The Four Bells*, Nick and Grahame were deep in discussion with Suzie Brush, the sexy student Phillipa correctly suspected her boss was most keen to bed before the end of the course and her friend, a pretty girl with long blonde hair named Beth Grafton who, like Suzie, worked as an assistant account director in a top London advertising agency.

Aided and abetted by Nick, Grahame had been teasing the two girls about an advertisement their agency had produced for a protein powder which claimed to enlarge the bustline.

'You both know very well that none of these damned potions advertised in women's magazines will make the slightest scrap of difference,' he commented. 'The only way for any girl to improve her bust is to exercise and improve her posture so as to make the most of what she's been given.'

'He's right, you know,' said Nick, as he passed round four large gin and tonics. 'And as my auntie, who sells bras in Selfridge's, always says, a good foundation will do wonders for your contours.'

Beth turned to Suzie and with an amused smile playing about her lips said: 'My goodness, doesn't this conversation show how true the old saying is about learning something new everyday. Tell me, Suzie, were you aware that not only Dr Johnstone, our beloved teacher, but also one of our own fellow students, Professor Armitage, possessed such expertise in health care?'

Suzie giggled and agreed: 'It's absolutely amazing, and I would never have guessed that either of them were medical men. Dr Johnstone, perhaps you could have a look at my elbow, I tripped and knocked it against the wall this morning and it still hurts a little.'

Grahame Johnstone was more than happy to enter into the spirit of the game and immediately replied: 'Certainly,

Miss Brush, if you'll come back with me now to my surgery and take off all your clothes, I'll be happy to give you a thorough check-up.'

It was now Nick's turn to chip in: 'No, don't go with him, Suzie, all the women say: "Thank you for coming so quickly, doctor" after Dr Johnstone has made a house call! I've a much better idea – come back to my surgery and we'll both take off our clothes before I start my examination.'

'Okay, boys, point taken,' said Beth. 'But although I know there have been as many claims for bust enlargement as there have been for hair restorers, this protein supplement really does seem to work. If it didn't, we wouldn't have taken on the account because it's not that big and the agency wouldn't want to court bad publicity.

'If you must know, I tried it out myself and as a matter of interest, the programme does include exercises which take into account what you both say. I followed the instructions and as well as wearing a well-fitting bra, every morning for two weeks I had to do the exercise which was doing the breast stroke swimming movement standing up twenty times, stretching the arms out in front, drawing in the abdominal muscles and stretching the arms backwards, keeping them level with the shoulders and bending the elbows, tucking them into the sides as far back as possible. Then I would drink a glass of milk mixed with a sachet of the protein formula.'

'And have your bust measurements increased?' enquired Nick.

'Yes,' she said earnestly. 'I can truthfully report that in just two weeks my bustline became firmer and fuller and had increased in size from thirty-three to thirty-five and a quarter inches.'

Nick shrugged his shoulders. 'Well, I can't argue against the facts, so I'll give in gracefully and accept that this stuff worked for you. Mind, I'm not convinced the protein does any good, it's the good bra and the exercise that did the trick.

'Not that you needed any extra inches, Beth. I have to say that any woman who is worried about the size of her boobs is silly. As someone in the business, I can tell you that fashions in shape change just as quickly as fashions in clothes – look at Twiggy for heaven's sake! She's got nothing on top yet she's the hottest model in Europe!

'So there's no such thing as the perfect pair of bosoms,' he added as he raised his gin and tonic to his lips. 'Cheers, everybody.'

Beth tilted her glass in acknowledgement and in a sweet voice replied: 'Fair enough, Nick, but I wish I had the rights to market some similar product for men. We girls might make ourselves unhappy about our tits, but you men are just the same about the size of your dicks. As far as most men I've known are concerned, their cocks come in just one size – too small!'

'*Touché*, pussycat! Every guy I know, and that includes me, would be happy with another couple of inches, especially when practically everyone else in the changing room seems better endowed than you!' confessed Nick with a short laugh.

Now it was Suzie's turn to enter the fray. 'But that's only because you're looking down at the other men's pricks from an angle which doesn't give you an accurate comparison,' she pointed out with a naughty wink at Beth, who nodded in agreement. 'And in any case, when they're on jack they all measure roughly the same.'

Grahame looked thoughtfully into his glass and murmured: 'I'm afraid that I don't entirely accept that, Suzie, we're not all built alike.

'Not that I make any claim to having any jumbo size tackle down below,' he added hastily.

'Damn! There goes another fantasy!' said Beth and all four of them roared with laughter.

'As my mum always says, God gave women a conscience and men their dangly bits,' said Beth, downing her drink. 'But as Suzie said, all your pricks are about the same dimensions.'

'No, that's not so,' said Grahame seriously as Nick called over to the bar for four more large gin and tonics. 'Take my word that there are some men who, how shall I put it, are blessed with what many would call those vital extra inches, although it isn't always something to be envied.

'I know this to be so from the first sexual experiences of a friend of mine called Desmond Brentwood who was known at school as DD, which stood for 'Donkey Des', and one look at him in the showers and you would have understood why he was lumbered with this nickname. All the boys were jealous of him although funnily enough, the first time he managed to get his girl friend Linda, who was in our class at school, to unzip his fly was the night of his sixteenth birthday party at his house before his parents returned home. He and Linda had been snogging and she'd heard us making rude remarks about Des's equipment and must have been feeling randy, because when Des suggested they slip upstairs away from the crowd, she decided to find out for herself if there was any truth in all these rumours.'

'But far from being turned on when his stiffie popped out of his pants, Linda was frightened by its size. She had given his hard-on an occasional feel through his trousers but had never before let him take it out, and when she finally saw Des's enormous eleven-inch erection, she was scared about letting this monster anywhere near her!

'It was all very frustrating for Des for he had thought he was in with a great chance of getting his first fuck when he had locked the bedroom door behind them, but alas, it was not to be. Linda wouldn't even let him slide his hand under her bra which she had done last time they had necked, and five minutes later they were back downstairs looking very gloomy.'

'The poor lad,' commented Suzie with genuine sympathy. 'Did he manage to persuade her to come back for a second look?'

Grahame chuckled as he shook his head. 'No, but it hardly mattered because he crossed the Rubicon only a couple of months later with Miss Grant, our new history teacher. She was only twenty-three and fresh out of college and somewhere along the line she must have heard about his massive tool, for the games master caught her sucking Des off in the changing rooms and reported them to the headmaster.'

'Dear me, how embarrassing! Nothing as interesting ever happened at my school,' said Nick as he gave a light-hearted wink at the girls. 'And presumably he hauled Des over the coals and sacked Miss Grant?'

'Not exactly, in fact the whole business was hushed up because Des claimed he had seen the headmaster having it away with Miss Grant in the back of his Morris 1100 one night when he was taking a short cut home through the local hockey club's car park. But the headmaster did change Miss Grant's timetable so that she taught the second year kids instead of our fifth form class.'

'Sounds like a fair enough compromise to me,' observed Beth thoughtfully. 'I'm sure that Des was hardly an unwilling participant, although I have to admit that if it had been the other way round and the case had involved a teenage schoolgirl having her pussy sucked by a male teacher, I would want the guy to be prosecuted.

'I suppose you men will think that's being unfair,' she

added, but neither Grahame or Nick would disagree with her.

'As a hard and fast rule, teachers shouldn't have it away with their students,' began Grahame before being stopped by Suzie who put a hand on his arm as she said in a disappointed voice which Grahame gauged was not altogether feigned: 'Oh no, does that mean that Suzie and I are safe from being molested by you after we go swimming this afternoon?'

The languages lecturer wagged a reproving finger at her as he went on: 'Suzie, you're jumping to conclusions, I was going to add that this only applies as far as kids are concerned.'

'So adult students over the age of eighteen are fair game,' interjected Nick with a grin. 'Phew, what a relief, there's hope for you yet, girls, although if for any reason his body is unavailable, don't forget that mine is always at your disposal, even if I can't offer you anything on the lines of Desmond the Dick, or whatever they called Grahame's old school chum.'

'Donkey Desmond,' Grahame corrected him and continued: 'and as a matter of interest, Des always said that when he went on holiday he didn't enjoy going down to the beach because people were always staring at the bulge in his swimming trunks, and what made him feel more uncomfortable was that men were worse than women.'

'Poor old Desmond, whatever became of him when he left school?' asked Beth and Grahame sighed: 'Good question, we lost touch a few years back but the last I heard he went into publishing as a travelling salesman. Someone told me that he was now the Southern area manager for one of the paperback publishers, but I can't remember which one.'

'Well, not to worry, let's toast poor old Des and his overgrown organ,' said Beth breezily. 'And then Suzie and I want to have a quick bite of lunch and get ourselves down to the beach. This place isn't on the Riviera and we have to make the most of this wonderful weather whilst it lasts.'

Nick rapped his knuckles on the table and said: 'Quite right, Miss Grafton, that's precisely what I had in mind when I ordered a lunch hamper for four from Signor Volpe at the Trattoria Veneziana in Lempert Street. I'll pick it up and I suggest we eat *al fresco* on a quiet little beach Grahame and I found the other day. It's under the cliff opposite the entrance to the new caravan park they're building just out of town on the Brighton Road.

'Will all those in favour kindly raise your hands?'

Four arms shot upwards and Nick carried on: 'Motion carried unanimously. Now the only difficulty is that it will be a bit of a squeeze for four of us to squeeze into my MGB.'

'No problem, Nick,' said Grahame promptly. 'I did a favour for Mr Ridout, the manager of the Langham Park, by taking his Sunbeam Alpine in for a service at the garage over the road. The mechanic said I could collect it at lunchtime and as Mr Ridout doesn't expect the car back till this evening, I'm sure he won't mind my using it this afternoon.'

'Great, so would one of you like to come with me and we'll pick up the grub. Oh yes, and on the way to the beach I'll have to pop into my hotel for a cossie and a couple of towels.'

'I'll go with you, Nick,' volunteered Beth, brushing the silky blonde strands of hair away from her face. This not only pleased Nick, who had been really smitten by the shapely, long-legged girl, but also Grahame whose lusty interest in the curvy Suzie Brush was obvious to all, and the lecturer was even more delighted when, as he looked to her for approval of this plan, Suzie nodded and said:

'Sounds like a super idea, Grahame, you won't mind driving me to our flat, will you? I must also pick up our swimming costumes. Beth, I'll bring along that nice string bikini for you.'

Beth gave her a thumbs-up sign. 'Thanks, Suzie, and don't forget the Ambre Solaire, we should get ourselves a great tan this afternoon.'

'I'll remind her,' promised Grahame as he looked up at the clock on the wall. 'Okay then, Suzie and I will meet you on the beach in about half an hour – and first of all I'll pop into an off-licence and buy us something to wash down our meal.'

'Wonderful, we'll see you later. Don't be too long, folks. Remember, the last one in the sea is a cissy,' grinned Nick as they finished their drinks and filed out of the bar.

The two cars pulled into a small cul de sac, which was handily situated only a hundred yards away from the steps down to the sea and sand, within three minutes of each other.

'Beth, can you ask Suzie if she could give you a hand with the hamper? I've a beach mattress and two deck-chairs to take out of the boot,' Nick explained as he hauled himself out of his car.

Beth snapped her fingers in annoyance. 'Damnation, I quite forgot about bringing something to lie down on. Oh well, we'll have to take it in turns to snooze on your mattress.'

'No we won't,' called out Grahame. 'Bill Ridout has left a beach mattress on the back seat which we can use. He's even got a foot pump as well so it'll only take a minute to blow it up.'

Once down on the secluded strip of fine sand, Suzie and Beth went into a cave to change whilst Grahame and Nick undressed on the beach, which was totally deserted as it was well away from the wide shores alongside the town's sea-front. By the time the girls returned, Nick had begun spreading out the goodies from Signor Volpe on paper plates the restaurateur had wisely provided, and Grahame was opening the first bottle of chilled white wine with the bottle-opener which Suzie had fortunately reminded him to buy from the off licence.

The two men were kneeling on the warm sand and Nick had just passed a small stack of paper cups to Grahame when Suzie and Beth reappeared, and his jaw dropped and his outstretched arm was temporarily frozen into a waxwork-like immobility as he looked at the shapely girls who were walking briskly towards him.

Both girls had changed into skimpy bikinis but Beth wore an especially daring creation in shiny pink, with the top half consisting of two small bra cups over which her creamy breasts spilled out, although he could see the outline of her thrusting nipples, whilst the pants were little more than a tiny triangle of material which scarcely covered her prominent mound and the strong waistband disappeared into the crack of her bottom, leaving her luscious buttocks totally bare.

Nick swallowed hard and his reaction was not lost on Beth who turned to Suzie and complained 'Honestly, I don't know why I let you persuade me to buy this bikini. It might be a genuine Ronnie Bloom model but it's really over the top. I wouldn't dare wear it on a public beach.'

'Don't be so daft, Beth,' Suzie retorted as they approached the men. 'You've got a stunning figure, so why not show it off? Tell you what, I'll bet Nick won't be able to take his eyes off you all afternoon.'

'Take my eyes off what, Suzie?' Nick called out and she replied: 'Beth's new bikini, would you believe that she's worried that it's too saucy to wear outside her own back garden.'

The two men scrambled to their feet and they chased the girls into the sea, and a happy Bernie Gosling could have told them that on this particular day the temperature of the water at Falmington was three full degrees warmer than the tepid waves of the Mediterranean around Cannes where, by an ironic coincidence, Nick's boss Alan Gottlieb was enjoying his annual two-week stay at the luxurious Hotel Martinez.

As Suzie had correctly predicted, after they had returned from their refreshing dip, during Signor Volpe's excellent lunch of pasta salads, tuna fish and cold chicken, Nick Armitage found it extremely hard to concentrate on anything but Beth's gorgeous body.

However, this did not exactly displease her, for she was similarly taken with Nick and welcomed his attentions. It had been more than six weeks since she had finally split from her boyfriend of almost a year, an account executive in the advertising agency in which she worked who had not kept contact when he accepted an offer to become the marketing director of a large West Midlands furniture manufacturer.

Nick thought he was getting the right vibrations as he sat chatting with Beth on one of the mattresses whilst Suzie and Grahame sat on the other and shared a copy of the morning newspaper, but he was not certain whether Beth was encouraging him to go any further.

God Almighty, the time, effort and money men spent trying to fathom out the wishes of the opposite sex, he thought grimly, when by stark contrast, simple animals with brains the size of walnuts seemingly got laid regularly without any trouble at all.

Beth was looking at him questioningly and at once he apologised: 'Beth, please forgive me, that was so rude not to give you my full attention. It didn't happen because I wasn't interested in what you were saying, but something

123

just suddenly struck me and I didn't take in your question.'

'That's all right, poppet, I could see you were lost in thought,' she said without rancour. 'What was on your mind?'

'I was just thinking how marvellous it would be to live the life of a beachcomber for a couple of months,' he fibbed as he ran a handful of golden sand through his fingers, although this thought had occasionally occurred to him. 'A small Greek island would suit me down to the ground, or maybe somewhere even further away in the South Pacific, far from the madding crowd.

'Don't get me wrong, I'm no hermit but a born and bred Londoner, and I know that after a time I'd miss all the noise and the bustle of the big city. Perhaps it's the crazy pace of life nowadays, rushing here and there, always on the go to follow the fashion, do this, go there, do that. Do you understand what I mean?'

'Yes, I understand what you're getting at, Nick,' she replied as she placed a towel over the rubber mattress and lay herself down on it with her head on the raised pillow. What was the name of that poet who wrote: *'What is this life if full of care, we have no time to stand and stare?'*

She moved over and invitingly patted the towel and Nick slid down beside her as he answered: 'W.H. Davies, and I only know because presumably like you I had to read him for 'O' Level, or I might have said Tommy Gemmell and taken the chance that I'd get away with it!'

'You would have been out of luck, because I know bloody well that Tommy Gemmell's the best full back in Britain,' she rejoined, nudging him in the ribs. 'Furthermore, my Dad's from Glasgow and I went with him to Lisbon in May to see Celtic win the European Cup.'

Nick threw up his hands in surrender and then, as he was about to speak, Suzie called out to them: 'Hey, you two lovebirds, do you fancy walking off that big lunch? Grahame and I are going to swim round the rocks and explore the next beach.'

He looked enquiringly at Beth who shook her head and murmured: 'I'm not that keen, though I'll make up the numbers if you want,' but Nick shouted back straight away: 'No thanks, Suzie, we'll stay here if you don't mind and keep an eye on our things.'

They waved as they watched Grahame and Suzie swim round the line of rocks which split up the beach, and then Beth moved herself over onto her tummy and asked Nick if he would put some suntan lotion on her back.

'My pleasure,' he said, reaching out for the bottle which was lying next to them on a towel.

Nick sat up to unscrew the cap and he poured out a little puddle into the palm of his other hand, but before he could transfer it to Beth's back, she brought round her arms and unclipped the catch of her bikini which she then slipped off and, raising her body so that he caught a fleeting glimpse of her bare breasts, threw the top onto the towel.

'That's better, you can dab some oil on now. I just don't want to have any white lines showing,' she explained as she sank back onto the mattress and Nick knelt down behind her.

Nick smoothed the oil onto her warm skin and with his fingertips massaged the brown, oleaginous liquid all over her back. 'M'mm, what a wonderfully light touch you have, Nick, you'd make a fine masseur if the rag trade ever shuts down,' murmured Beth, but his hands began to tremble when she added: 'but please don't neglect my bottom. The main reason why I agreed to wear this bikini was that I would be able to expose my bum cheeks to the sun.'

'Leave it to me,' croaked Nick, his voice breaking with

lustful passion as his prick swelled up swiftly and immediately made an alarming bulge inside his swimming trunks whilst he oiled the soft flesh of her deliciously rounded backside with both hands, one on each bum cheek, as he sat back on his calves between her parted thighs.

When he had finished, Beth moved herself over and told him to lie down next to her. 'There's just about room for two if we snuggle up together,' she said softly. 'Now, would you like me to rub some oil on your back?'

Nick slid down on his front, his stiff cock pressed between his tummy and the mattress as he passed the bottle of oil to Beth as he wriggled himself into a comfortable position. Beth was equally expert in smoothing her hands sensuously across his back and Nick closed his eyes in quiet bliss. But he was soon rudely awakened when he felt her hands tug down his tight-fitting costume over the swell of his buttocks.

'Hey, what are you up to?' he protested, but Beth only nibbled his ear and whispered: 'Lift up your hips, there's a good boy, so I can pull off these silly trunks and I can rub some oil onto your bum.

'Don't be shy, Nick, you'll find it so relaxing to stretch out naked on a secluded stretch of beach like this and listen to the waves roll in,' she declared as he complied with her instruction, and she rolled his trunks down to his feet to enable Nick to kick them free.

'Now isn't that better?' she asked as she slipped herself down beside him. For reply, he turned towards her and as their faces were drawn together as if pulled by the most powerful of magnets, their eyes closed and their mouths crushed together in a lusciously passionate kiss.

Nick held her tight and pressed the length of her soft body against him, kissing her lips, her face, her throat and she clung to him, her head thrown back as his mouth moved inexorably down her neck to the ripe fullness of

126

her bare breasts, and his lips closed over her hardening strawberry nipples.

Beth responded by grinding herself against Nick's throbbing erection and then, after first tugging off her tiny bikini pants, she wrapped her long legs around him, pulling him over her and with her hand she opened her love lips with one hand and with the other she guided his straining shaft inside her moist love channel.

He growled with desire as he pistoned his prick deep inside Beth's honeypot and she moaned with ecstasy as Nick pumped in and out of her juicy cunny, arching her back upwards to meet his fervent thrusts, and he drove home again and again as she urged him on, closing her feet together at the small of his back to force every last inch of his meaty staff inside her.

'Oooh, you're so *big*! God, I'm coming, I'm coming! Y-e-s-s! Y-e-s-s!' screamed Beth as a powerful orgasm forced its way through her body and the shivering force of her climax set off the ringing of an alarm bell in Nick's mind.

'Beth, is it okay for me to come inside you? I don't think that I can hold out much longer,' he panted as he plunged even further inside her clinging wetness, reaming the far walls of her clinging cunt as their pubic hairs matted together.

'Yes you can, darling, don't worry, I'm on the pill,' she gasped, lifting the anxiety which had cast a temporary cloud over the proceedings, and Nick continued to ride his rigid rod in and out of her sopping crack until his own climax was upon him and, with a hoarse cry, he slammed his twitching tool inside her as his cock spurted out a fierce fountain of sticky spunk, sending Beth off again into a wild little series of electric spasms of joy.

He felt his cock slowly shrinking as, still inside her, Nick held the trembling girl close to him and stroked her long silky hair. Then he gently pulled his glistening shaft out of her pussy and Beth rolled him off her and over onto his back.

'I'm making the towel all sticky,' he murmured in her ear.

She slid her hand across and slicked her fingers up and down Nick's still semi-stiff shaft and he began to harden as she murmured: 'So is your cock, my poppet. I'd better clean it up for you.'

Holding firmly on to his pulsing prick, Beth pulled herself across him and dipped her head down to rest on his thigh.

'A-a-r-g-h!' he gurgled as she stuck out her pink tongue and swirled it all over his uncapped knob, washing his helmet with her saliva as she ran the tip of her tongue around the rim whilst she gently manipulated his balls through their hairy wrinkled sack. Then she opened her mouth wide and started to suck vigorously on his throbbing pole, moving her head down in a regular rhythm as Nick pressed his hands lightly on her head and happily surrendered himself to the blissful sensations in his groin.

Now Beth lapped her way along the ultra-sensitive underside of his twitching tool, and Nick groaned with delight as he felt his straining staff being bathed inside the warm wetness of her mouth. She concentrated upon his knob, sliding her tongue to and fro over the smooth skin as she lovingly caressed his cock and balls until, shortly, a tribute of frothy seed gushed out of his helmet and she squirmed with delight as she gulped down Nick's creamy spunk with great enjoyment.

She licked off a final blob before letting her hand fall from his fast deflating shaft and she slumped back on the mattress and they hugged each other whilst Nick rained a short series of small, sensuous kisses all over her quivering body.

'Let's stay like this for a while,' she whispered as he ran his fingers along her spine and down to the crevice between the cheeks of her backside. 'Well, at least until Suzie and Grahame come back. Actually, I wonder whether they have been doing the same as us.'

'Good luck to them if they have,' commented Nick with a lazy grin. 'But they should have taken their mattress with them. Making love on the sand or in the sea sounds all very exciting but I would imagine that it can also be darned uncomfortable!'

'Tut-tut, where's the romance in your soul?' teased Beth as she gave his dangling shaft a friendly little tug before curling herself up around his body, and they lay entwined as they allowed the bright rays of the afternoon sun to warm their bodies, which were already glistening from their frenetic erotic escapade. 'Mind, after knowing Suzie for two years, I'm sure she and Grahame will have already put it all together one way or the other.'

'Yup, and knowing Grahame for just two weeks, I wouldn't bet against it,' grunted Nick as he kissed the perky nipple which was only an inch away from his mouth, but although he felt a slight sirring in his crotch, he declined to take things further and very soon the conversation ceased and they dozed contentedly in each other's arms.

Meanwhile, as Beth and Nick had rightly surmised, Suzie and Grahame were only six hundred yards away on a similar but smaller stretch of sand, with their naked bodies locked together in an erotic encounter.

As their tongues lashed sensuously together in a passionate, open-mouthed kiss, Suzie wished they had taken their mattress with them for she did not want to get her hair covered in sand, and she voiced her concern to her would-be lover.

Grahame thought swiftly and then muttered with a

gleam in his eye: 'Sure, I quite understand, Suzie, but there's an easy solution to this problem. I'll lie down on my back and you can ride up and down on my thick boner. Now how does that grab you?'

Suzie frowned and pretended to mull over the pros and cons of the idea in her mind. But then the gorgeous girl giggled and she said as she disentangled herself from their embrace: 'Aren't you a good boy to be so unselfish! Yes, it's a perfectly splendid idea.'

He threw his arms around her and they sank down together, but Grahame made sure that he was the one to lie with his back upon the slightly bumpy flat bed of sand. He gave his cock a quick rub until it stood almost up against his flat stomach, but Suzie took his hand away and said: 'We've plenty of time, so let's first enjoy a nice *hors d'oeuvre* before tucking in to the main course.'

'By all means,' he agreed, lying back and parting his thighs to allow Suzie to kneel between them, and she tossed back her long strands of light brown hair before slowly lowering her head towards his rock-hard, pulsating prick. Grahame gasped and his heart began to pound when her teeth scraped the tender flesh of his bell-end whilst she drew his shaft between her rich red lips, and he shuddered all over when before his very eyes he saw Suzie cramming his entire nine-and-a-half-inch shaft into her mouth down to his crinkly public hairs, and he could feel his stiffstander sliding past her epiglottis on its way down her throat.

To his immense delight, Grahame discovered that Suzie was an expert fellatrice who was going to give him the best sucking off of his life. As she lovingly palated his prick, the lecturer felt his balls swell under the soft caress of her hands and he let out a low growl as Suzie's wicked tongue lashed itself against his quaking truncheon and waves of delirious pleasure rolled through his body.

After less than two minutes, although Grahame tried as hard as he could to prevent it, he could feel his jism rising from his balls, but although she heard and understood the meaning of his choked sob of anger, Suzie continued to suck on her fleshy lollipop and with a huge groan, Grahame shot his spunk inside her mouth and Suzie swallowed his jism, smacking her lips at the taste of his tangy essence.

When Suzie finally finished milking his cock, she let him pull his shrunken member out of her mouth and Grahame's head drooped down as he inhaled a couple of deep breaths as he recovered his senses.

'Didn't you enjoy that?' she asked him with a note of reproach in her voice and he looked up at her and grinned: 'Is the Pope Catholic? Of course I did, you silly girl, it's just that it'll take a wee while till I'm ready to continue.'

He bit his lip as he remembered that earlier in the day he had said much the same thing to Philippa Farthing after he had fucked her doggy-style in his study, but Suzie was unfazed by his admission and replied: 'Fine, there's no hurry, we don't have a train to catch and I'm sure that Beth and Nick are quite happy to be on their own,' she said reassuringly. 'Anyhow, I'd be glad of a little rest myself.'

Suzie sat down in the sand and Grahame put his arm around her shoulders and for five minutes they sat and chatted quietly about her progress in his French class.

'You're doing really well, all you need is a little more confidence,' he told her. 'Just don't be frightened of making a mistake, the important thing is that you're capable of expressing yourself and of being understood.

'Sure, you're bound to make the occasional grammatical howler but as you probably know, most French people are very proud of their language and I guarantee that a

French-speaking client will be far more receptive to anything you say in a slightly broken French than in the most perfect English,' he concluded, although his concentration was then disturbed when Suzie lay back with her head in her hands and she parted her thighs as, with a wicked smile, she enquired: 'But am I making myself understood now?'

The lecturer swallowed hard and passed his hand in front of his face. 'I think you are,' he muttered hoarsely as he swivelled himself across her to lie on his front between her legs where he was given a close view of Suzie's cunny lips peeping through a deliciously fluffy muff of chestnut pussy hair.

'Oh yes it's perfectly clear to me what you'd like me to do,' he breathed as Suzie smoothed her hands over her breast and flicked her large red nipples between her fingers.

'M'mm, I see you've got the message,' she murmured as he leaned forward and kissed her pouting pussy lips. But before Grahame could begin to lick out her honeypot in earnest, Suzie suddenly turned round and, easing her weight on her hands and knees, she thrust out her peachy bum cheeks towards him and Grahame slid his hand gently into the crevice between her buttocks.

Grahame's prick had now risen smartly to attention and as he allowed his forefinger to slip between her rubbery love lips into her moist quim, he passed his other arm around the lovely girl and caressed her curvy, uptilted breasts and rubbed his palm against her stiffening nipples.

'Message received loud and clear,' he breathed when Suzie reached backwards and held out her hand in which there lay a small tube of sun-tan oil. She turned her head round and said: 'I though we might need this so I popped it inside my bikini before we left Beth and Nick.'

He wondered at first what Suzie had in mind but he was

very happy to oblige when she dropped her voice and whispered: 'I have a fancy to be bum-fucked, darling, you will oblige me, won't you?'

'*Mon plaisir, jolie mademoiselle*,' said her French teacher thickly as he smeared a liberal amount of oil onto this rock-hard organ.

He went to work with a will and the oil eased a path for his cock to slide slowly inside the tightness of her back passage, and Grahame inserted himself to the root of his shaft as Suzie's buttocks wiggled lasciviously against his belly and the lovely girl moaned as she took his weight and her slender frame rippled beneath him as his cock sawed in and out of her superb backside.

Then he withdrew slightly and pressed home again, and Suzie yelped with pleasure as she felt his balls slapping against the backs of her thighs and her gorgeous bottom responded to every shove as he jerked his hips to and fro in frenetic rhythm.

'Oooh, that's fantastic,' she breathed as the purple dome of Grahame's cock shunted in and out of her bum-hole at a great pace. But Suzie was in no hurry to feel his spunk drench her rear dimple and she called out: 'I don't want you to come too quickly. Stay still inside my arse for a little while before you start fucking me again.'

With a great effort, Grahame held himself still with his cock pulsing furiously inside its tight sheath, then counted to twenty and slid his arms around the trembling girl and massaged her creamy breasts. Suzie squealed as he let one hand fall in order to stroke the hard nub of her clitty at the top of her pussy slit whilst his prick pounded its oily passage between the polished white orbs of her glorious backside.

He worked his cock back and forth until Suzie began to shake with the force of an approaching orgasm, and then he finger-fucked her cunt faster and faster until she cried out: 'Yes! Yes! I've come!' and with some relief he relaxed and his shaft spouted a flood of sticky spunk which warmed and lubricated Suzie's rear.

Panting heavily from this erotic exercise, the sated lecturer fell forward onto her, but he quickly hauled himself up and placed one hand on the small of her back as with an audible 'pop' he uncorked his cock from her bum.

Suzie snuggled herself into the crook of his shoulder and said with a sigh: 'Grahame, can I tell you a secret?'

'Yes, of course you can,' he replied idly and she kissed his cheek and said: 'Promise you won't tell?'

'Cross my heart and hope to die if I do,' he swore gravely which made her giggle as she went on: 'Well, there must be something in the air around Falmington, because I've just realised that it was on this very beach just three years ago that I had the most wonderful fuck with Barry, my boyfriend.'

Grahame was amused and yet slightly irritated by Suzie's confession. He looked down at her pretty face with his lips in a lop-sided smile and commented: 'Is that a fact? So you wanted to come back here to try and recapture those magic moments?'

Suzie shook her head. 'No, because I'm not certain whether it was here or a little further down the coast. Anyhow, to be strictly accurate, Barry first fucked me in my bedroom at the hotel.'

'Who was this chap? Someone you met down here?' he asked, fighting back what he realised was an unreasonable jealousy.

'No, it wasn't a whirlwind holiday romance, I'm not the sort of girl that jumps into bed only a few hours after meeting a man for the first time,' she remonstrated, reaching down to give his cock a little angry pull. 'As I said, this all happened three years ago when I was only

134

seventeen and Barry and I were both virgins. He lived round the corner from our house and we'd been going out together for about six months. At the time, I was still at school doing my 'A' levels and Barry was working in a local factory as an apprentice tool-maker.'

'Highly appropriate,' Grahame murmured and received a second tug on his cock for his pains.

'We'd gone in for some heavy petting,' she continued with a saucy grin, 'but we'd never actually fucked, although we'd come too close for comfort a couple of times and I knew that one day we probably would go over the top. Although I'm sure I would have made Barry wear a rubber, I wanted to make sure I was fully protected so I decided to go on the Pill. I knew I'd have no trouble with our family doctor, Dr Abigail, because she's a nice, sensible lady who could see that I was good and ready for my first fuck.'

'Good for her,' observed Grahame and she nodded and went on: 'This was about six weeks before I was due to go with Mum and Dad to Falmington for a summer holiday. Jimmy, my young brother had gone off to a holiday camp and my parents insisted that they wouldn't allow me to go away with other girls until I was eighteen.

'I think they were surprised when I said I'd be pleased to go with them to Falmington. Mind, what I *didn't* tell my parents was that just before we left London, Barry promised that he would show up on the first weekend of our stay. And sure enough, he booked himself into a boarding house near our hotel and called me up on the Friday night to make plans for the next day.

'On the Saturday morning the weather was fine but I pretended to have a headache when Mum and Dad asked me if I wanted to join them on the beach, and told them that I'd prefer to stay by myself and have a snooze at the side of the hotel pool.

'Of course, as soon as they left the hotel, I telephoned Barry and he came over to see me. I sunbathed in my bikini whilst Barry went swimming and when I watched him climb out of the water, I couldn't help feeling aroused as I gazed at him, taking in how his dark curly hair fell over his eyes, the rippling muscles of his upper arms and the way his tight swimming trunks hugged his tight little bum and moulded the swell of his cock and balls.

'I could feel a warm ache beginning to throb in my pussy and I decided at that moment that I would let him seduce me. I threw him a towel and as he dried himself I beckoned him to come closer to me and said softly: "How would you like to come up to my room and take off your wet trunks there?"

'His eyes sparkled as he whispered back: "I should say I would, Suzie, especially as I don't have another cozzie to put on!"

' "Never mind, you can always wrap a pair of my knickers round your prick," I said as he helped me to my feet. "Listen, they're a bit stuffy here so I'll go in first and you follow me in later. I'm on the fourth floor, room forty-eight. Knock four times on the door so I know it'll be you and not the maid or Mum coming back early to see whether I'm feeling better."

'Barry winked at me and muttered: "Good thinking, Batman, as it happens I promised faithfully that I'd send my sister one of those naughty seaside postcards, you know the sort, so I'll slip my shorts over my trunks and nip out and buy one at the little shop over the road, scribble something to her and pop it in the letterbox outside the hotel. I won't be long, not more than five minutes."

'The naughty boy then gave me a long, hard kiss before trotting off to buy his postcard, and my legs began to tremble so much that I could hardly walk through the hotel to the lift. When I reached my room I shut the door and leaned against it. Then I put my hand inside my bikini and felt my pussy, which was already wet. My clitty was now hard and throbbing so I unhooked the catch on my bra and pulled off my panties and threw myself down naked on the bed.

'Gasping for breath, I ran my fingers through my soaking thatch, fluffing up the hair and teasing it away from my crack, and then I splayed two fingers downwards in a vee and spread open my cunny lips along the length of my slit with one hand, whilst with the other I plunged two fingers in and out of my cunt. I closed my eyes and pictured Barry pulling down his trunks and seeing his thick shaft spring out ready for action.

'This made me so randy that I quickly came in a kind of frenzy, tossing my head from side to side as my hand buried itself inside my love channel, rubbing over the swollen hood of the clitty until I brought myself off with a great all-over shudder.

'As I lay panting on the bed, I heard the lift door open and moments later there were four sharp raps on the door. "Come in, Barry, it's not locked," I called out, forgetting that I was still absolutely starkers, so it was just as well that it was indeed Barry who slipped into the room!

'At first he did not see me so he looked round the room after he had shut the door. But when he did see me his jaw suddenly dropped and he gulped hard as he stood stock still as if transfixed. For a fleeting second I was puzzled but then in a flash I realised that I was in the nude and that this was the first time Barry had ever seen me stark naked.

'He kicked off his sandals and pulled down his shorts so he stood trembling in his swimming trunks, and Barry's eyes roved over my body as he said in a hoarse whisper, his voice cracking with emotion: "God Almighty, Suzie, you really are so beautiful."

'I said nothing but smiled at him as he ran his hands up the sides of my arms and my titties began to tingle whilst the air from the deep breaths he was taking whistled across my stiffening nipples, making them stand up rigid like two little red corks. Then, Barry extended his thumbs to rub them over my breasts as again he ran his hands up and down my arms.

'I had time for just a brief glance at the bulging swell in his trunks before Barry threw himself upon me and kissed me with such passion that I almost fainted away. His lips were wet and soft and my pussy began to moisten again as I felt his tongue exploring every inch of my mouth whilst his hands roamed freely over my breasts, stroking, cajoling and squeezing as we squirmed from side to side with our legs wrapped round each other so that our bodies were pressed together from head to toe.'

'It was when he pressed my hand down to feel that huge bulge between his legs and I felt the outline of his throbbing pulsing prick that I knew that the time had come for Barry to fuck me. I let myself be swept along by the tide of passion which was engulfing us and rolled down the top of his trunks till I could see the top of his knob peeking out above the waistband, and Barry helped me tug his trunks over his hips and thighs and his huge, purple-domed shaft rose up proudly from between his legs, exposing his wrinkly pink ballsack which I took gently into my hand.

'Now he slid his hand between my legs and I trapped it there, clasping my thighs together whilst I bent down and for the very first time I kissed his cock whilst with his free hand Barry caressed my head, running his fingers sensuously through my hair. I opened my mouth and sucked in his knob between my lips. Remember, I'd never done this before and I wasn't sure whether I'd like it, but once I'd had that first nibble and suck on his hot cockflesh, I knew that everything was going to be all right.'

Grahame let out a short snort of laughter and said: 'And I'll bet that your friend Barry had no complaints either!'

'No, he certainly didn't!' she chuckled as again she pulled his prick, and this time Grahame's tadger twitched and began to stiffen as she slid her fingers up and down its swelling length. Suzie kept her hand around his hardened shaft, squeezing his cock deliciously as she went on: 'Anyhow, whilst I was licking his knob, I released his hand from my pussy and he began to finger-fuck me, dipping three of his fingers in and out of my sopping honeypot. This thrilled me so much that I sucked even more eagerly on his prick and I crammed as much of his massive shaft as I could inside my mouth and I sucked and slurped on his cock until it began to pulse, and then Barry shot his load and my mouth was filled with a great gush of his sticky spunk. Funnily enough, it never occured to me not to swallow his jism and to Barry's great delight I gulped it all down.

'This made me come myself and I sprayed his fingers with cunny juice as I continued to suck on his still stiffish shaft. Very soon his cock was rockhard again and he pulled out his prick from my mouth and rolled on top of me. We were both panting with lust as his body sank down on top of me.

'I parted my legs and grasped hold of his glistening wet truncheon and gave it a final rub as Barry guided his knob towards my cunt, and I shivered with anticipation as I felt his smooth helmet lodge between my yielding cunny lips, and the thought flashed through my mind how sensible I'd been to go on the Pill, for now I could relax and enjoy myself without any worries.

'But when Barry tried to push his prick further inside my cunt, even though my pussy was now soaking wet, my cunt had not been stretched enough to accomodate such a thick cock and I let out a hurt little cry as he attempted to thrust home. Immediately he withdrew and looked anxiously at me and asked: "Oh my darling, does it hurt very much?"

' "No, I'll be okay," I panted and this time I opened my pussy lips with my fingers, stretching my cunny as he slid his prick inside me. This did the trick and when he panted: "Is that any better?" I whispered back fiercely: "Oh yes, yes, yes, fuck me, Barry, fuck me, you big-cocked boy!"

'My rude reply reassured him and he placed his lips on mine and sucked my tongue inside his mouth as his prick forced its way in, and with only a few more slight twinges of discomfort, the remainder of my hymen was torn away and my cunt held Barry in a tight, juicy grip. This spurred him on to pump faster and deeper inside my love channel, drawing his palpitating prick backwards and forwards with each shove, and my liberated cunt clung to his cock with every delicious movement. Then his body stiffened and I felt my own orgasm rushing up as he clenched his teeth and oh! I'll never forget that magic moment when he spurted his spunk inside me. It sent a rush of burning liquid fire coursing through my cunny, and with each throb of his trembling tool more spunk drenched my pussy till I thought he would never stop, and I now reached my own climax and screamed out with sheer animal lust as ripples of the most ecstatic pleasure rippled out of my sated cunt.

'Barry covered my face with kisses as he rolled off me and lay on his back with his arms outstretched and a beatific smile on his face, for remember this was also his first time as well as mine. We lay in each other's arms much like we are doing now, and after a while his cock began to thicken and sway between his thighs as I fondled him, but we decided to wait till the afternoon to do it again.

'And I remember we went by bus along the road out of town to one of these quiet stretches of beach and made love again there, but I'm not sure whether it was this one or perhaps where we were with Beth and Nick,' she concluded with a little frown as she tried to recall the exact location.

'Bloody hell, just thinking about that first fuck makes my pussy tingle,' she said dreamily, and then she glanced up at Grahame and saw that he had been stimulated so much by both her story and her sensuous frigging of his cock that he was in even more desperate need of relief.

Suzie was more than happy to oblige Grahame for her needs were similar to his, so wordlessly she took her hand away from his straining shaft and lay on her back, parting her legs and spreading apart her love lips with her fingers to expose the glowing red chink of the entrance to her cunt.

Grahame leaped across her and directed the tip of his glowing helmet between her squishy love lips and joyfully pushed forward, embedding his prick inside her to the root.

'Oooh, you've filled me up so nicely! Now fuck the arse off me, you randy rascal!' she gasped and, nothing loath, he started to slew his shaft in and out of her juicy cunt, cupping her luscious bum cheeks in his hands as his throbbing boner slid backwards and forwards at a tremendous pace.

Suzie came almost immediately, sinking her teeth into his shoulder as the initial tremors of a wonderfully fulfilling orgasm began to gather force inside her groin, and she screamed with ecstatic joy as her climax exploded and to cap her delight Grahame ejaculated a stream of sticky jism, further creaming her seething cunt, and as they writhed around in a mutual frenzy of lust, a white slick of spunk dribbled slowly down between the cheeks of Suzie's rosy bottom.

When their bodies finally ground to a halt, Suzie scrambled up to her feet and ran towards the water, calling out for Grahame to follow her.

'Come on in for a dip, it's as warm as toast,' she shouted back as she splashed her way into the clear blue water. Grahame sighed as he rose to his feet, for he would rather have taken a rest after their short but vigorous fuck. Nevertheless he lumbered down to the water's edge and Suzie came and, taking hold of his hand, pulled him further into the sea.

'Come on, let's swim over to where we came from and see how Beth and Nick are getting on,' she suggested, and she lay on her back and kicked up a frothy fountain of water which splashed all over him. 'Last one there has to buy the first round of drinks in the bar tonight.'

'Hey, that's not fair, I'm a rotten swimmer,' he protested as Suzie took off, expertly ploughing through the waves with a smooth breast-stroke action which had won her a place in her school swimming team, and although Grahame was not such a poor performer in the water as he had suggested, Suzie easily kept in front of him as he struggled to narrow the distance between them.

They were so intent on their race that it was only when Suzie stopped swimming and stayed still, treading water as she shouted: 'I've won! I've won!' that Grahame suddenly realised that they had both left their costumes behind on the beach and that he and Suzie had been swimming in the nude.

'Hold on a minute, wait for me!' he gasped out as Suzie began to wade ashore. 'Suzie, haven't you forgotten something?'

She shook her head as she waited for Grahame to get

nearer to her. When he reached her side he chuckled: 'We're both bollock naked, my dear. Now you might well look like Venus rising from the waves to Nick, but Beth might be embarrassed to see my John Thomas swinging from side to side as I walk towards them – and come to think of it, I'll also feel more than a bit flustered!'

Suzie threw back her head and laughed and her beautiful breasts were thrust out firmly as, raising her arms to squeeze some water out of her hair, she said: 'So we are! But don't let it worry you. As you say, Nick won't mind at all and honestly, you don't have to worry about Beth. She's seen quite a few cocks in her time, believe me, and one more or less won't matter at all.

'Anyhow, you silly boy, can't you guess what they've been up to whilst we've been away? I'll bet you that round of drinks that they're also stark naked like us!'

Taking his hand firmly in hers, Suzie tugged her apprehensive languages teacher towards the shore. In for a penny, in for a pound, muttered Grahame as he let himself be pulled by the pretty girl towards the beach mattress where Beth and Nick were lying together, dozing peacefully in the sunshine.

'Ah ha, I told you so,' said Suzie triumphantly as she pointed to the couple who, as she had forecast, were both totally naked. Beth was lying on her tummy and Grahame looked with a freshly aroused lust at the adorably luscious cheeks of her backside whilst Suzie gazed with interest at Nick's thick shaft which was dangling over his right thigh.

'Hello there, you two lovebirds, we're back,' announced Suzie but the only reaction to their presence was a sleepy grunt of greeting from Nick whilst Beth flopped an arm lazily upwards and murmured: 'Hi, folks, did you enjoy your little walk?'

'Very much, thank you,' replied Suzie who then turned to Grahame and said: 'Darling, would you be an angel and get my camera? I want to take some photographs but I've left it in the boot of your car.'

'Sure, but I'd better slip on something first or I'll get arrested,' he grinned and Suzie threw him over a towelling robe Nick had brought with him. 'Nick, you don't mind if Grahame borrows your robe, do you?'

'Not at all,' Nick murmured and Suzie noticed that his eyes were still closed against the bright sunlight.

A wicked smile spread slowly across her face and as she helped Grahame into Nick's robe, she whispered: 'Shush now, don't say anything more about the camera when you come back and I'll take some photographs of these sleeping beauties which will be a darned sight more interesting than the usual set of holiday snaps!'

She winked at Grahame who chuckled as he rummaged through the pockets of his trousers for the keys of his car and replied: 'Okay, Suzie, I shan't be very long.'

Grahame returned in less than five minutes clutching a Rollei Automatic in one hand and a yellow chrysanthemum in the other. 'I didn't realise that you were into photography,' he commented as he passed it over to Suzie. 'A friend of mine is a sports photographer on the *Daily Mirror* and he uses one of these for work.'

'It's not mine, one of the guys from the agency studio offered to lend it to me and said he would develop any shots I took whilst I was down here,' said Suzie as she took the camera from him. 'But tell me, who gave you that lovely flower?'

'A couple of girls are dishing them out to all and sundry at the caravan park across the other side of the road, with leaflets about a Flower Power night at Eric's Club this evening,' he said as he presented it to her and he added regretfully: 'I should really have taken another one for Beth.'

Suzie looked at him and then leaned forward and

whispered something into his ear. Grahame looked shocked and put a hand to his cheek as he said: 'Oh, come on now, you can't be serious!'

She nodded her head vigorously and urged him on. 'Yes I am, Grahame, don't be bashful, darling. I promise you that Beth will simply adore being woken up in that way.'

For a moment he hesitated but then he shrugged and as instructed, he knelt down in front of Beth who was lying with her thighs slightly parted so that Grahame could see the slit of her cunny peeking through the silky bush of pussy hair. He looked back at Suzie who hissed: 'Go on, Grahame, do what I told you, tickle her bum with the chrysanthemum!'

'Okay, okay,' he said softly and he let the yellow head of the flower brush inside the crevice between Beth's beautiful bum cheeks. The blonde girl opened her legs wider and murmured: 'M'mm, that's nice, very nice,' and when she looked round to see what was tickling her sensitive secret crannies, she smiled and went on: 'Wow! I've heard of flower power but this is ridiculous!'

She sat with her eyes closed and she thrust out her gorgeous, perfectly rounded bottom cheeks towards him, slightly lifting her body so that Grahame was able to flick the blossom against her pussy crack.

'M'mm, that is *really* nice, you're making me feel very randy, you naughty boy!' she cooed softly. 'I love being taken from behind.'

The silence was broken by the whirr from Suzie's camera as she continued to click away as Grahame passed his hand against the majestic smooth cheeks of Beth's bum, and his cock started to rise as he let his hand linger on her rear dimple before passing his fingers below to feel the soft, wet lips of her squishy cunt.

'Carry on, teacher,' she murmured as she pulled her arm back to grasp hold of his burgeoning erection. She slicked her fist up and down his shaft and then let go as she placed her hands flat on the mattress in order to raise her bottom even higher. Grahame's shaft strained at the leash at the sight of Beth's bum-hole and rubbery cunny lips. In a flash he lined up the broad, uncapped knob of his cock and squeezed it between her buttocks and into her squelchy quim with one smooth thrust.

Below him Beth bucked as she savoured the honeyed movement of his pulsing prick inside her juicy love channel, and her pants of pleasure now awoke Nick who sat up and watched the performance with lecherous surprise. Suzie saw his prick thicken and swell and she put down the camera and sank down between his legs, cradling Nick's blue-veined shaft in her hands.

'What's going on here?' asked a bewildered Nick and quick as a flash Suzie answered. 'I don't really have to tell you, do I?' and she lowered her head and took the mushroom crown of his cock between her lips, sucking the juicy sponginess whilst she released one hand to squeeze his tightening balls. She flicked her tongue under his swollen helmet and bobbing her head in a sensual rhythm, she fucked his throbbing member superbly with her suctioning mouth, licking and lapping whilst Nick jerked his hips in time with her rhythm, arching his back upwards as she held his quivering cock firmly between her tightly compressed lips.

Beside them, Grahame had his hands clamped on Beth's quivering buttocks and he pressed his thumb into her bum-hole as he fucked her with great style, pistoning his prick in and out of her delicious cunny, his balls slapping against her thighs as he shunted his cock forward, pulled it back and thrust it in again.

Both men were soon teetering on the brink, their climaxes overlapping as Grahame shot his load into Beth's clinging cunny whilst Suzie rolled the tip of her wet tongue around the velvety skin of Nick's shaft, feeling it pulsate as though it possessed a life of its own.

'I'm coming, I can't stop!' Nick gasped and as she fondled his tight, sperm-filled balls with her soft fingers, he sprayed her mouth with a stream of frothy jism which Suzie gulped down, licking all round his knob to gather up stray splashes as the spongy textured helmet softened under her tongue.

The energy and enthusiasm of the two beautiful girls apparently knew no bounds for after a refreshing dip in the sea, Beth lay back on the beach mattress and demanded that Grahame brought her off by licking out her pussy and, though delighted to oblige, it occurred to the lecturer that if things continued in this vein much longer, he'd have to be brought home in an oxygen tent!

But not just yet, he murmured to himself as he settled his lips inside Beth's fluffy blonde bush, not until his cock utterly refused to play any more games . . .

# CHAPTER FIVE

## *A Very Naughty Night*

As the beeps sounded to signal seven o'clock, Murray Lupowitz swung over an arm and switched off the radio in his room at the Langham Park Hotel. Then he slumped back on his bed, yawned and contemplated whether he should heave himself up and start to memorise the list of twenty-five new Spanish words Signora Salinas had asked students in her Spanish class to learn by the beginning of tomorrow afternoon's lesson.

Fuck it, he decided, I'll get up at half past six tomorrow morning and sit down quietly for an hour with the vocabulary sheet before breakfast, though if his plans for this evening came to fruition, he would not see his bed again till the early hours.

As he had written to his cousin David back in Brooklyn, Murray was having somewhat mixed feelings about staying on in Britain after his year-long stint in London with Chelmsford and Parrish. On the one hand, he would be glad to return home and see all his old friends, but on the other, there was great compensation in the raging affair he had been enjoying since the spring with Denise Cochran.

Murray had been looking forward to spending time with Denise in Falmington, but to his annoyance, the business management course which he had recommended so highly to her had been scheduled for the mornings whilst his Spanish classes took place during the afternoons. And not only did this mean that the only time he and Denise could meet during the day was during a hurried lunch at the pub or at the college canteen, but Denise especially was occupied with a substantial work-load of study for the evenings.

Furthermore, due to a mix-up in the accounts department of Chelmsford and Parrish, Denise's deposit for her room at the Langham Park had not been sent and her reservation had been cancelled. Although she had been able to book into a very comfortable single room at the Royal Windsor instead, this hotel was a quarter of a mile away and so far it had not been possible to spend more than three nights with Denise.

And as if this were not enough, these three nights had been spoiled by the fact that he had to smuggle himself out of her room by six in the morning so as to avoid any trouble, for at the Royal Windsor as in all other hotels in Falmington, there was a house rule that guests in single bedrooms were strictly forbidden to entertain any overnight guests.

Any guest wishing to bring in a sleeping partner could usually overcome any normal scruples by the pressing of ten shilling notes into the appropriate palms, hoteliers naturally had more serious economic objections to letting two people stay overnight in a single room.

He breathed deeply and tried to banish the irritation from his mind by thinking of the joys which might lie ahead later that evening. Along with all the other members of his class, he had been invited by his ravishing, dark-haired tutor to a party at the College.

'I do hope that everyone will come along and, of course, you can all feel free to bring a guest with you,' Signora Maria Salinas had said to them earlier in the week. 'I will

supervise the preparation of some typical Spanish food by
the canteen staff, and thanks to a friend of mine who
works at the Spanish Tourist Office, we will have plenty to
drink as he will come down from London with two cases of
Rioja. Also, Pepe y Francesca, the flamenco dancers on
the bill at the Queen's Hall theatre, have agreed to come
along after their performance tonight and demonstrate the
flamenco to us. So I'm sure we will all have a wonderful
time.'

Later that evening he had telephoned Denise and
invited her to the party but she had shaken her head and
said: 'Murray, I'm awfully sorry, I'd love to go with you
but Mr Teplin has set us so much homework this week
that I'm going to have to stay in and study every night till
the weekend.'

Of course he had been upset that despite his trying to
change her mind, Denise had remained adamant that she
could not afford to take a single night away from her
books, but over the previous few days Murray had been
slightly distracted during his classes by Lucy Gunther, a
pretty Canadian girl with whom he paired up in conversation classes and during the ten-minute tea break in the
middle of their three-hour afternoon sessions.

'We North Americans must stick together,' Murray had
said gravely when he had first recognised her accent in the
classroom. Since then he had always sat next to the
gorgeous nineteen-year-old who told him during a tea
break that she was taking a Spanish course before she left
Britain, where she had been staying for six months with
some of her mother's relatives. Unlike Murray, she was
not planning to return home but would instead make the
long journey down to Uruguay where she would stay
during the South American summer with her relatives
who lived in Montevideo.

'My father's parents were German, but when Hitler

came to power, my grandparents decided to emigrate,' Lucy explained when Murray had asked her how she came to have relatives so far away, and he had sighed: 'I could never understand why more German Jews didn't leave in the nineteen-thirties. My mother's sister and her entire family were murdered in a concentration camp during the war.'

'One of the reasons is that they had nowhere to go,' she had replied as Murray took two cups of tea from the canteen counter and they made their way to an empty table. 'The British kept as many Jews as they could out of Palestine because they didn't want to offend the Arabs, whilst the Americans only doled out a very few entry visas.

'But in fact my grandparents weren't Jewish. They left Germany because they hated Hitler who they thought was a madman who would destroy all of Europe. Fortunately, my grandmother had a wealthy cousin who had built up a big import-export business in Uruguay since he left Germany after the First World War and this made it easier for them. My Dad had his fourteenth birthday on board ship bound for Montevideo and he met my Mom at the International School there. From all accounts it was love at first sight and they married whilst they were studying together in the United States.'

'And I hope they lived happily ever after,' said Murray with a smile.

'Yup, Dad's a research physicist and he got a good job in Toronto where my mother wanted to settle because her family live round there, my brother and I came along and that's it really,' she twinkled as they sat down at a table near the window. 'But since my grandparents died, we haven't kept in touch very much with Dad's relations in Uruguay. That's because Dad's forgotten a lot of his German so he can't communicate too well with his older relatives and, as he was taught in English at the International School, he only has a smattering of Spanish and can't do much better with the younger Gunthers! They all learn English at school but I thought that if I'm going to stay with them, it's only right that I should be able to speak at least a little bit in their own language.'

Murray smiled as he lay back on the bed with his hands behind his neck, thinking of how luscious Lucy had looked in her white vest and short skirt when he had come into college that morning and he had seen her playing netball on the court by the car park. He had waited until the game was finished and then he had asked if he could pick her up and take her to Signora Salinas's party this evening. She had readily accepted his invitation and had given him the address of her boarding house, and Murray said he would pick her up there at half past eight.

And although she had given no real indication that she might be interested in anything more than a chaste kiss on the dance floor, Murray sensed that Lucy could possibly be ripe for something more sensual if he could persuade her to let him drive up Middleton Hill to the clearing in the trees around Tucker's Point where, during the day, visitors could have a marvellous view of the coastline and where by night a peeping tom would have had an equally superb view of lovemaking couples in the row of cars parked there if he were able to wipe the steamed-up windows.

What the hell, it was not as if he were engaged to Denise, he reasoned to himself. They were very close friends and hopefully she would visit him in New York next year, but he was a free agent and if the chance of a good fuck dropped in his lap, he certainly was not going to spurn it.

His thoughts were interrupted by a ring on the telephone and he reached over and pulled the receiver towards him, hoping that it was not Denise on the line saying that she had decided to go to the party after all.

'Murray Lupowitz here,' he said crisply and he heard a soft, American-accented voice reply: 'Hi, Murray, this is Linda here.'

'Linda? I don't know anyone called Linda,' he said and then he swung his legs off the bed as he suddenly realised who it was calling him. 'Hey, hold on a minute, that's not, no it can't be—'

'Who can't it be, Murray?' giggled the sexy female voice.

'Linda McNichol, is that you?' he cried out delightedly. 'Hey, what the heck are you doing over here? I suppose you *are* in England, aren't you?'

'I sure am, honey, I flew into London this morning and your nice secretary gave me this telephone number when I called your office,' she answered and then she blew a kiss down the line. 'Does that remind you of anything, you naughty boy?'

Murray laughed out loud for the last kiss he had received from Linda McNichol had been on the saliva-coated shaft of his cock as he was pulling his cock out from between her rich, glistening lips. Linda was an actress and one of Murray's steadiest girl-friends back in New York, though that didn't mean too much, for despite her profession being even more overcrowded than in Britain, Linda's agent had managed to secure several good rôles for her within touring theatrical companies and even in the occasional off-Broadway production.

'How could I ever forget?' he said with a broad smile on his face. 'It's great to hear from you, Linda, have you managed to get some work in London?'

'Yes, that's one of the reasons why I'm calling you. Would you believe that I've landed my first movie rôle,' she answered. 'Sheldon Barnett wrote the screenplay

154

about three American girls who take a vacation in Europe, and Dick Cavendish is directing. You know, the guy that won an Oscar nomination for *Tamara's Wardrobe* last year. We'll be shooting in London, Paris and Rome for the next seven weeks.'

'Wonderful! Hey, we must get together and celebrate,' Murray enthused but then his face fell as he went on: 'Uh, there's just one problem, Linda, my secretary might have told you that I'm here on a summer school course and I won't be able to come up to London till the weekend.'

'Oh no, have I got to wait as long as that to see you?' said Linda reproachfully and she gave a sexy little chuckle. 'The guy at reception told me you're only sixty miles away. Haven't you got a car with you? It would only take you a couple of hours to come back to London and see me. I'm staying at the Hilton Hotel on Hyde Park Corner.'

Murray gnawed at his lip as she continued: 'Believe me, I'd make it worth your while, darling. I can't wait till the weekend to be fucked by your big fat cock. I've been thinking about it ever since we landed and here I am all alone, feeling very randy and you're not here to welcome me to London.'

Linda paused and then Murray listened to her give a throaty chuckle and mutter: 'I'm lying naked on my bed, Murray, and I'm getting so hot thinking about your thick hard cock, I'll just have to bring myself off without you. Yes, that's what I'm going to do. I'm slipping my hand between my legs now and I'm rubbing my pussy.'

Murray's cock began to twitch as he heard a series of little sighs down the line which proved that Linda was telling the truth. He breathed heavily and Linda muttered: 'Murray, are you sitting on your bed too? And are you also naked?'

'Yes, it so happens I am,' he gulped and she panted:

155

'Oh, Murray, have you got a hard-on? Go on, rub your cock whilst I play with myself. M'mm, I can imagine that lovely stiff shaft of yours throbbing away and I wish I were there to swirl my tongue round your knob.

'I'm squeezing my nipples between my thumbs and forefingers, watching my breasts rise and fall. Now I'm reaching down to play with my pussy. M'mmm, that's better, that's much better! Oh God, I wish it was your mouth down between my legs and it was your tongue licking my pussy and your teeth nibbling on my clitty. I'd do anything to have your cock inside my wet cunny, feeling it pump in and out of my juicy honeypot. My wet cunt is more than ready for you, I'm slipping three fingers inside it, sliding them to and fro . . . Ooooh! My fingers are deep inside and I'm shaking all over and all the pussy juice is dripping down my thighs. I'm dabbing my titties with cunny cream and cupping a tittie to my mouth to lick it off . . . Christ, I'm coming and you're not even here. A-a-a-h! There I go . . .'

By now Murray was holding the telephone in his left hand whilst his right hand was travelling up and down his quivering erection and Linda now purred: 'Murray, are you still there? Have you been wanking that stiff thick prick of yours? Haven't you come yet? Think about licking me out whilst I suck your cock, lover boy. Or how about a tit-fuck? You've always loved my breasts, haven't you? Listen, darling, I'm squeezing them together and you can rub your cock on my hard little red nipples.

'Come on, cover my titties with jism,' she said in a husky whisper and Murray let out a low cry as a fountain of spunk spurted out from his cock. Linda must have heard him for she now purred: 'Oh, you sexy boy, what a lot of spunk! Wouldn't it be nice to rub it all over my soft creamy breasts! You can do, you know, it won't take long to drive back to London.'

He was sorely tempted to take her up on her offer but he could hardly let Lucy Gunther down at the last minute, especially when presumably Linda would not be too angry if she only had to wait till tomorrow night to have him in her bed. So he blew a kiss into the phone and said: 'I'd love to, Linda, you know I would, but I've made arrangements for tonight which I can't cancel. But how about tomorrow night? I could be with you by half past eight.'

'I don't know about tomorrow night, Murray,' she said doubtfully. 'I have a press call scheduled for six o'clock and then I'm going out for dinner with Crystal Clarke and Sheila Williams, the other two girls in the movie.'

'Well, suppose I come round later, say around eleven o'clock?' he persisted. 'I don't have any lectures till the afternoon so I wouldn't have to rush back to Falmington.'

'Okay then, Murray, but if I'm not in when you arrive, you'll have to wait for me in the lobby.'

'No problem, Linda,' he replied. 'Thanks for calling and look forward to seeing you tomorrow.'

Murray slammed down the receiver and punched the air with his fist as he heaved himself to his feet and padded into the bathroom. There was ample time for a leisurely bath before he had to meet the luscious Lucy Gunther, and he was buoyed up by the certain knowledge that even if he didn't score this evening, the following night he would be fucking the ass off his sexy playmate from back home.

As Murray lay back in a warm bath in his room at the Langham Park, Lucy Gunther was about to listen to a warning about their landlady's good-looking twenty-year-old son Raymond from Jacqui Burgess, another student at the summer school who was also lodging at The Grange Boarding House.

'You'll hardly believe me, Lucy, but I promise you I'm

not exaggerating,' said Jacqui. 'I came back from the college this afternoon about an hour earlier than usual,' looking round to ensure that there were no other guests in the Residents Lounge. 'The front door was open but there was no-one at the reception desk. So I took my key from the board and went upstairs to my room.

'As I was climbing the stairs, I thought I heard a noise coming from my room so I stopped. For a moment I thought about running downstairs and calling Mrs Thompson, but then I recognised Raymond's voice coming from behind my door.'

'Goodness, what was he doing there?' breathed Lucy and Jacqui smiled grimly. 'Well, you may ask,' she replied, looking again round the room to check that they would not be overheard. 'I opened the door as quietly as possible and poked my head round to see what he was up to – and Lucy, you'd never guess in a hundred years what I saw! Raymond was lying naked on my bed, fondling his throbbing erection with one hand and in his other he had a pair of my panties which I'd left on a chair, and he was pressing them against his nose as he wanked himself off.

'He was so lost in his fantasy that he hadn't seen or heard me come in and I didn't know what to do as I stood there, mesmerized by the sight. He started to moan: "Oh Jacqui, please let me lick your pussy, open your legs and I'll bring you off with my tongue. That's the ticket, lie down on my face so I can see your lovely slit. I'll open it out with my fingers and I'll lap up all your cunny juice!"

'Then whilst he chewed away at the crotch of my knickers he jerked his hand up and down his cock and, with a loud groan, he started to climax. I could see the first spatters of spunk bubble out of his bell-end and run down his shaft and when he began to slick his hand faster and faster, a huge spurt of jism gushed out and made a tiny white pool of sperm on his belly.'

Lucy slowly exhaled a deep breath and said: 'Heaven's alive, did you let him know what you'd seen?'

'Uh-uh, I just quietly stepped back onto the landing and closed the door. I'm not a prude and between ourselves, I get quite turned on by seeing a lad playing with himself. That probably comes from when I was sixteen and into heavy petting with Maurice, my first boyfriend. I was really aroused when I was jacking him off but one night he said to me: "Ouch! You're not doing it right, Jacqui," and this made me angry so I said: "Well, you can toss yourself off, mate!" – and he did! It seems I was squeezing him too hard and though I was a little upset at first, I was fascinated to watch how he pumped his hand up and down his prick.

'Anyhow, since then, I've always been excited by seeing my boyfriends masturbate,' Jacqui concluded. 'Even young Raymond, though I could do without him using my panties whilst he did it! I think I'll have to tell him that I saw him pulling his pud earlier on, and that in future, if he wants to wank, he should do so in the privacy of his own bedroom. And come to think of it, he can buy me a new pair of panties from Marks and Spencer as I don't fancy ever wearing again the pair he was stuffing into his mouth this afternoon!'

Lucy laughed as she looked up at the clock on the mantelpiece. 'I must get ready for this party I was telling you about,' she said as she stood up and walked towards the door. 'Thanks for telling me that funny story and, tomorrow morning, don't forget to let me know what happened when you decide to confront Raymond.'

She went upstairs and changed into a slinky sleeveless black minidress and she was just putting on her lipstick when she heard footsteps coming up the stairs. There was a knock on her door and she recognised Raymond's voice as he called out: 'Miss Gunther, there's a gentleman waiting downstairs for you. Can I give him a message?'

'Thank you, Raymond – please tell him I'll be down in a couple of minutes,' she called back, and Lucy repressed an urge to giggle as she thought of what he might say if she added: 'and don't you dare come into my room and wank into my panties, you naughty boy.'

Murray was in the hallway when she came down the stairs. 'Wow! You look stunning!' he said sincerely as he took her hand as they made their way to the front door. 'And ready on time, too! For that you earn a silver star, Lucy. I'm not a terribly impatient guy but I hate kicking my heels at eight o'clock when the girl's told me to be round at seventy-forty-five.'

She acknowledged the compliment with a smile and they chatted away about the course and their fellow students whilst Murray drove to the college. The party was a great success and along with the others they ate and drank their fill of paella and sangria.

Signora Salinas switched on a record player and they danced together on the improvised dance floor. 'M'mm, this sangria has quite a kick, hasn't it?' said Lucy as the music of the Beatles gave way to a smoochy melody.

'That it has,' remarked Murray as he clutched hold of her soft body round the waist. 'Sangria is usually made up of red wine, sugar, lemon juice and iced soda, but I have a notion that someone has laced tonight's potion with brandy.'

'I enjoy drinking wine at parties, it relaxes me nicely,' said Lucy as she threw her arms around Murray's neck and pressed herself against him. 'But I don't like smoking pot which seems to be all the rage these days.'

'It is, but I'm not sure it's such a terrible thing to do. Some doctors say pot doesn't do you as much harm as alcohol,' Murray replied, but when he saw a disapproving frown form on her brow he added hastily: 'but then I

160

haven't tried it myself because I don't smoke at all, although God knows I've been to enough parties where you could smell the marijuana a mile away. Smoking pot is very widespread amongst the chattering classes in London. One of the editors at the publishers I worked for in London smoked pot in the office occasionally and nobody batted an eyelid about it.'

'Oh sure, I don't see why people shouldn't be allowed to do what they want, especially in the privacy of their homes,' she agreed as they gently bumped against a couple kissing passionately on the now-crowded dance floor. 'But I distrust men who light up on a date. If a guy says he wants to get high before we make love, I'm always suspicious that it's because he feels it won't be good enough without that extra stimulus – and as far as I'm concerned, that's a goddamn insult, insinuating that my body isn't enough to turn him on.'

Murray gulped as he felt Lucy grind her groin tightly against his straining erection. 'At least you don't appear to need any pot to turn you on,' she murmured in his ear.

'Of course I don't, Lucy,' he replied in a fierce whisper as he lightly kissed her on the lips. 'I was turned on from the moment I saw you coming down the stairs from your room when I came round for you tonight.'

'You really mean that, Murray?' she said softly and he gasped as Lucy slid her arms down from the back of his neck and rubbed her palms against his chest. Then she opened a button on his shirt and slipped her hand inside his shirt until she found one of his nipples and began to touch it, playing with it gently between two fingers until she felt Murray shiver with excitement.

She drew slightly away, moistened her lips with the tip of her tongue and then came closer to him and licked his lips. Instantly they parted for her and she kissed him hard, darting her tongue quickly round the inside of his mouth, drawing quickly away again. Murray was now oblivious to anything except the feel of this beautiful, sexy girl in his arms and he pulled her back for he desperately wanted to continue the embrace, but Lucy resisted and said : 'Not here, Murray, not here.'

'Let's go then, I was thinking of driving you to Tucker's Point to see the view over the coast.'

She smiled and placed her finger on his lips. 'Murray Lupowitz, you're a big fibber! You might have wanted to take me to Tucker's Point but don't try and tell me that you ever planned to get out the car!'

His face coloured a bright shade of pink as he wrapped his arms around her and confessed: 'I plead guilty, your honour, but don't be hard on me. After all, it's my first offence so I throw myself upon the mercy of the court.'

Lucy looked at him gravely for a moment and then she said : 'Well, after due consideration, I sentence you to take me back to my boarding house for a nightcap after we thank Signora Salinas for making this party. Do you accept this judgement or do you want to appeal to a higher court?'

'Oh no, I wouldn't appeal even if you added a hundred dollar fine!' he laughed as he took her hand and guided her off the floor to Signora Salinas who was standing by the bar.

'Must you leave so soon?' she asked when Murray said he and Lucy were off home. 'The flamenco dancers will be here very shortly.'

'Another time, perhaps,' said Murray politely. 'But Lucy has an early class tomorrow so we'd better make tracks.'

Ten minutes later, Lucy was unlocking the front door of The Grange and now it was her turn to lead Murray by the hand as they crept quietly up the stairs to her room. Once inside, she switched on the lamp at the side of her bed which cast a shadowy light over them. They sat down on the bed and Murray looked at her questioningly as he picked up the transistor radio on the bedside table.

But Lucy shook her head and said: 'No, don't put it on, the noise might disturb one of the other guests. Anyhow, I'm not that keen on background music – it distracts me and I like to concentrate on what I'm doing. If I hear a favourite song whilst I'm kissing you I'll start listening to it and that would spoil things for both of us.'

'Well, I certainly wouldn't want that to happen,' he breathed as he set down the radio and encircled the gorgeous girl in his arms as she tilted her face upwards towards him. Their lips met in a passionate kiss and their tongues burst through into each other's mouths and their bodies fused into an eager, sensual tangle of limbs as they lay on the bed, tearing off their clothes until Murray was naked and Lucy was wearing only a tiny pair of black silk panties. Murray was riveted by her graceful voluptuousness as her soft, rounded breasts commanded his eyes, their nipples rosy and pointed.

At his urgent, whispered request, Lucy lay down and arched her back as with trembling hands Murray tugged down the shiny little panties over her hips. He caught his breath at the sight of her prominent pouting love lips in the midst of her tightly curled nest of pussy hair. He ran his fingers over her lips, then down into the dark, flowery tangle, then out again, finding her hands and guiding them to the thick stiffness of his cock which was quivering upwards with his knob pointing towards his navel.

Her nimble fingers fondled his thick, smooth-skinned penis until he gently disengaged them and he knelt between her outspread thighs, tucking his face between them, and Lucy shuddered as he tongued the outside of each love lip in turn. She was already wet and slowly he inserted his thumbs between her lips and ran them along her juicy crack, opening her cunny up so that he could tongue her clitty which had now popped out of its shell.

'Y-e-s-s-s! Y-e-s-s-s!' she panted as a delicious cum made her twist from side to side, and Murray steadied her with his hands as he lapped up the flow of cuntal juice.

'Now you lie back, I want to ride you,' she breathed and he obeyed without question, slithering down as Lucy scrambled up to kneel between Murray's legs. She bent over him and began to kiss his face, first on his lips and then back up onto his forehead and down onto his eyelids. A violent shiver swept over Murray's body as she moved further down, blowing on each of his nipples as she slid down the bed, using her hands and mouth, tickling, licking and rubbing and he groaned with desire as with his steel-hard shaft pulsating in her hand, Lucy crouched over him and guided his prick into the clinging wetness of her cunt.

'God Almighty, that's fantastic!' he gasped as she drove herself down so quickly that Murray felt as though his embedded member now belonged to Lucy as much as it did to him. She moved her lithe young body over him, sliding up and down on his throbbing tool and he rubbed his palms against her stalky nipples as she rode faster and faster on his cock, gyrating her hips as Murray now grabbed hold of her luscious buttocks whilst he jerked his body upwards to meet her downward thrusts. Her sticky love channel slipped up and down his raging cock and the sensations of her cunny muscles nipping his shaft were so strong that Murray climaxed sooner than he would have wished inside Lucy's dark-fringed honeypot.

His jism shot out in a fierce fountain and drenched the walls of her love channel and Lucy let out a short scream as she thrust her body forward, rubbing her big, elongated nipples against his hairy chest as she exploded into a body-wrenching orgasm.

When the force of her climax subsided, Lucy slithered down to lie beside him, but there was hardly room for two on the narrow single bed so Murray moved himself up onto his knees and looked down at her gleaming curves as Lucy lay back, her arms flung out, her breasts flattening widely. Murray kneeled over her face and let his cock and balls hang over her lips. Lucy's tongue snaked out, licking and lapping the underside of his shaft until it stiffened, and he carefully lowered his hips so that she was able to suck his knob and he eased himself gently inside her mouth.

Then he twisted himself round, licking his way along her body until his face was again buried inside her bushy thatch, and their bodies bucked and twisted as they lay there, sucking and lapping and drinking in each other. He pulled her thighs up round her face and squeezed her firm bum cheeks which made her giggle and twist delightedly.

'Two can play at that game, mister!' she giggled and began delivering light slaps on Murray's buttocks with her open palms which sent a warm glow throughout his body. Somehow, he managed to postpone his orgasm, but Lucy came again, moaning and jerking her hips as she thrust her quim into Murray's ever-open mouth.

They changed positions and Murray turned round and sat astride the lissome girl, placing his glistening prick in between her spread breasts and she gathered them together in her hands, making a narrow channel for his shaft to slide excitedly backwards and forwards whilst he tweaked her rubbery red nipples between his fingers.

Murray could hold on no longer and out of the tiny hole in his helmet spurted three powerful jets of jism which shot across Lucy's breasts into a pale shining pool of spunk, and smaller spasms followed until he was drained and his shaft started to shrivel inside the supple sheath between her bosoms.

He sank his face down on the pillow but then his head

jerked up when from behind him he heard a husky female
voice say with feeling: 'If it were something you were
drinking at that party tonight which had this effect on you
two, I hope you've brought back some of it for me!'

Startled by the intrusion, Murray looked round to see
the shapely figure of Jacqui Burgess, Lucy's fellow lodger
at The Grange, standing in the open doorway. She was
wearing a pale blue silk robe, the sides of which parted
when she shut the door behind her and walked forward to
reveal the long lines of her gleaming thighs.

'How about playing a game for all three of us?' added
Jacqui as, without waiting for an answer, she slid the robe
off to reveal her lush nude body. 'We agreed to share and
share alike, didn't we, Lucy?'

'Oh yes, I don't mind at all – so long as Murray doesn't
mind,' said Lucy sweetly as she looked up to Murray for
confirmation that he had no objections to Jacqui joining
them.

Not surprisingly, Murray was pleased to welcome
Lucy's friend and grinned: 'Be my guest, though it's only
fair to tell you that I've come twice already and so my cock
will be out of action for a while.'

Jacqui's face fell as she heard this disappointing news,
but she shrugged her shoulders and said: 'Not for too
long, I hope. I'm Jacqui Burgess, by the way, Murray.
Perhaps you remember seeing me up at the College. I'm
also at the summer school, taking the business administration course with the famous Mr Bruce Teplin from the
London School of Economics.'

This is unreal, thought Murray, as he shook Jacqui's
outstretched hand. I'll wake up in a minute, all frustrated
when I find out this has only been a wonderful dream. But
when he pinched himself on the arm he realised that this
was no dream as he politely replied: 'Hello, Jacqui, I'm
afraid there's not much room on this bed, but please feel

free to take my place whilst I sit in that easy chair and take a little breather.'

'Thank you,' said Jacqui as she dropped to her knees at the side of the bed, her large breasts jiggling sensually as her hand slid up between Lucy's smooth legs and began to rub sinuously between her thighs. This made Lucy sigh with delight and she threw her head back in ecstasy as her pretty friend's palm gyrated wickedly upon her hairy pussy.

Murray dragged himself up to make room for Jacqui and she took his place whilst he moved to the small armchair at the side of the bed. Meanwhile, Lucy offered no resistance as Jacqui explored her firm, full breasts which she cradled in her hands, teasing and caressing until the nipples stood up like two tiny red soldiers. And as she felt Jacqui's lips close around her tittie, she closed her eyes and sighed, gurgling with pleasure when Jacqui slipped first one and then two fingers inside her wet pussy whilst the heel of her hand rubbed her clitty which was already protruding through her love lips like a hard little walnut.

Lucy's hands now gripped her back as they pressed their slippery bodies even closer together, and Jacqui ducked her head downwards to the moist, silky hairs of Lucy's prominent pubic bush and with a sudden dart plunged her pointed tongue in and out of the hirsute curly mound.

'M'mmm, you naughty girl,' smiled Lucy as she rocked gently from side to side as Jacqui's tongue revelled in the wet smoothness of Lucy's love channel, licking, flicking and sucking as one of her arms snaked around Lucy's waist and the other sped downwards to her own pussy, finger-fucking herself at a quickening speed to meet the pace of Lucy's approaching climax.

Looking at this erotic scene excited Murray and he rubbed his shaft furiously in order to bring his tired cock back to life. However, not even the sight of Jacqui and Lucy's luscious naked bodies could raise more than a flicker of interest in his groin, so he stopped his unsuccessful attempt to achieve a hard-on and sat bent forward, his hands on his knees, to watch the culmination of Jacqui's frigging.

He did not have long to wait for as Jacqui's tongue gave a long sweep of her juicy cunny walls, the girl's body started to tremble with the force of an on-coming orgasm. Her hips bucked, her back rippled and then from Lucy's tingling pussy gushed a stream of tangy love juice which flooded Jacqui's mouth and ran down her chin as she diddled herself to an equally pleasurable climax.

Jacqui lifted her head from the padding of Lucy's hairy pussy and looked somewhat smugly at Murray as she said: 'I don't want to sound rude, but it's just as well that we girls don't need a cock to bring ourselves off, isn't it? Let's face it, there are very few men who can match my feminine finesse when it comes to sucking pussy.'

Murray shrugged his shoulders but Lucy heaved herself up on her elbows to disagree with her friend. 'I think that's a wee bit unfair, Jacqui,' she argued. 'I'll agree with you that generally speaking girls are more skilled at eating pussy, but even though I adored the way you sucked my nipples, I must admit that I preferred to have Murray tit-fuck me with his big, thick stiffie. You must have seen how he rubbed his shaft on my breasts and then how I gobbled his cock whilst his balls brushed against my titties.'

'Oh, I don't say that there's anything wrong with a nice, meaty cock!' protested Jacqui as she swung her body onto one side, pressing against Lucy so that their breasts and pussies were pressed closely together. 'Perhaps my view is coloured by the fact that it took me a time to really get off by fucking. When I was sixteen I was into heavy petting with Ken, my boyfriend. It felt nice to have him touch my breasts and play with my pussy whilst I rubbed his cock, but when I finally let Ken fuck me, it didn't honestly do very much for me.

'I never had a proper orgasm with Ken but when I went to secretarial college I met Johnny Colmer, who was learning shorthand because he was a trainee journalist and needed to learn shorthand. Incidentally, if you read the *Daily Sketch* you might have seen his by-line, he's the paper's chief crime reporter. Well, he and I got very friendly and one night my parents had gone out and we were canoodling on my bed and, of course, he wanted to go all the way. The smooth-talking so-and-so finally persuaded me and once we were both undressed he lay me down and began to kiss me all over.

' "You just lie there, I'm going to do all the work," he whispered as he guided his knob between my cunny lips. Very slowly he slid his thick cock into me and very slowly he pulled it out. Then he did this again, and then a third time, creating a kind of huge suction from my cunt. Of course Johnny had diddled my pussy with his fingers but this was my first proper fuck and I was getting more and more excited.

'As my movements became more and more agitated, he reached under me and popped the tip of his little finger up my bum. At first I tensed up but then he gently began to rub around the rim and told me to relax. Then he started to fuck my cunt at a quicker pace, pushing his cock in harder and faster and at the same time he jabbed his finger into my bum, only about half an inch. He worked his finger and his prick simultaneously and then alternately; whilst his tadger was all the way inside, his finger was out to the first knuckle and then he would plunge it inside as he withdrew his throbbing tool. This must have lasted for about a minute until I felt this tremendous force pulsing out from my pussy and I just exploded. It was my first orgasm and it knocked me for six – not that I'm complaining!

'Since then I've found that I can reach a climax without my lover fiddling with my bum but I do have them more consistently when he does,' concluded Jacqui.

Murray cleared his throat and said: 'It's always best to say what you would like your partner to do. If he or she doesn't like that particular thing, okay, fair enough, but there can never be any harm in asking.

'As far as I'm concerned, Jacqui, I'd be delighted to oblige you,' he said, as at last he felt his cock begin to stiffen up and, in a trice, he was on the bed with the two girls who squealed with delight as he kissed each of them in turn, wiggling his tongue inside their mouths as their hands met together, clasped around his rigid shaft.

Jacqui scrambled onto her knees and pushed out the delectably rounded cheeks of her backside towards Murray as Lucy whispered: 'Would you like to fuck Jacqui from behind whilst I suck your balls?'

He nodded and Lucy bent forward and twirled her tongue over Murray's cock, washing his helmet as she took hold of his rigid rod and teasingly planted the purple knob in the crevice between Jacqui's glorious buttocks, and planted the tip of his bell-end against the yielding pink lips of her cunt.

'Here we go, Jacqui, brace yourself, darling!' said Lucy as she pushed three inches of Murray's quivering shaft into her friend's juicy honeypot. Then she squirmed down so that her head was underneath his dangling balls and she started to lick and lap his wrinkled pink ballsack as Murray built up a rhythm, pushing and pulling his glistening prick in and out of Jacqui's clinging cunny. Her bottom wriggled sexily as he drove deeper and deeper, pumping and thrusting as she reached back and spread her cheeks as Murray fucked her with long, sweeping strokes of his sinewy prick. He felt his cock swell even more inside her pulsing love channel as Jacqui drove her body backwards against the power of his own forward thrusting, and they both bounced back from each encounter, meeting each fresh onslaught with little yelps of delight.

Murray was on his knees with his hands clasped on Jacqui's gleaming bum cheeks and Lucy tried frantically to keep his balls inside her mouth, but the pace of the fuck was too great and she had to open her lips and let his tightening ballsack go free. Then she remembered what was guaranteed to give her friend an orgasm, so she slid her finger into Jacqui's arsehole and the girl cried out: 'A-h-r-e! That's it! I'm there!' as she trembled all over as the first waves of a delicious climax coursed through her body, and then all the tension drained out of her as though a great tide had been undammed and she fell back, sated by the powerful force of the juddering climax which Lucy had coaxed out of her.

However, Jacqui soon recovered and said friskily to Murray: 'Thanks for the lovely fuck, I hope you enjoyed it as much as I did. Now, how about a final screw for Lucy?'

'Out of the question, I'm afraid,' said Murray hastily. 'I couldn't raise a stand now, not if you offered me a thousand dollars.'

'You poor boy, have we exhausted you?' she said with a wicked smile. 'Never mind, you go back to the chair and Lucy and I will have to make do with a vibrator. Luckily I left it in here the other evening, so I don't have to go back to my room.'

Jacqui opened the small drawer underneath Lucy's bedside table and triumphantly brought out her dildo, which was about nine inches long and ingeniously shaped like an erect penis, complete with a helmeted crown and raised veins running along the length. She switched it on but there was only a low buzz and no movement from the vibrator.

'Damn, I forgot that the battery was so low,' she muttered as she rubbed the head against Lucy's pouting pink cunny lips. 'Sorry darling, we'll just have to make do with what we've got.'

'Never mind,' said Lucy, opening her legs wider and displaying the gaping flushed chink of her cunt to Murray as Jacqui began to slide the instrument along the length of Lucy's slit, taking good care to rub her clitty at every stroke, and Lucy squealed with joy as Jacqui plunged the thick imitation cock in and out of her silky fringed cunt in a series of slow, deep strokes.

'Is that nice?' she enquired and Lucy nodded her head as the dildo sank out of sight, and Murray craned forward to see it reappear coated with juices from her honeypot.

Lucy drew some great heaving breaths as she concentrated all her energies on clasping and unclasping her cunny muscles around the dildo, and she twisted and bucked until she achieved a climax although it was not as forceful as her previous orgasms and she panted: 'Thanks for trying, Jacqui, but I think my pussy is telling me that it needs to go to sleep!'

'As does my cock,' groaned Murray, tenderly fingering his circumcised shaft. 'My God, you two girls are the most marvellous fucks but it's time for me to throw in the towel.'

As Murray kissed Jacqui and Lucy goodbye, Denise Cochran – the girl whose presence attracted Murray to study at Falmington as opposed to elsewhere – was sitting alone in her room at the Royal Windsor hotel. She was rightly feeling very pleased with herself for not only had she resisted Murray Lupowitz's invitation to accompany him to a party at the College, but she had even refrained from reading a letter which she recognised from the handwriting on the envelope had been written by her flatmate, Jenny Forsyth, until she had finished her essay on *Capital Expenditure and Cash Flow* for Bruce Teplin.

Only when she had finished did she slit open the envelope and take out the letter from Jenny which she lay down on the bed to read. Denise guessed that the letter would mostly be about her boss, Pete Bailey, but Denise wondered whether the affair was still going hot and strong or whether it might now be floundering. It took her only a quick glance to be assured that all was well and a wide smile formed on her face as she read:

*Dearest Denise,*
*How are you enjoying life at the seaside? I hope it's not all work and no play and that Murray is looking after you as nicely as Pete is looking after me. He took me up to Manchester on Tuesday for a fashion show by one of his biggest suppliers and we had a wonderful time there. The only problem was that we couldn't stay the night because one of the girls who works with me in the boutique is off on holiday and so I had to get back to open up in the morning.*

*We caught the last train to London which was barely a quarter full and we had no difficulty in finding an empty, first-class compartment. I sat next to Pete and leaned against him as the steady rocking motion of the train made me jog against Pete, and he kissed the top of my head and said: 'It's been a very long day, Jenny, would you like me to give you a massage?'*

*'I'd love one,' I replied as I took off my coat and I moved across the seat slightly so that my back was facing him. His fingers started out on my back and shoulders, then gently slipped to the sides of my breasts and discovered that I was not wearing a bra*

*under my jumper.* His hands dived under my jumper
and he let the tips of his fingers lightly brush against
the underside of my bare breasts, which soon had me
panting as my nipples swelled up with desire.

At Pete's request, I lay down on the seat and he knelt
on the floor and slid his hand between my legs,
running his fingers deftly over my inner thighs until I
was fairly shuddering with lust. I arched my bum
upwards and he pulled off my panties and his hand
returned to begin a slow, sensual massage of my pussy.
He caressed my bush, causing my cunny muscles to
spasm with pleasure. He laughed softly as he felt me
shudder and stroked the lips of my cunt, and I pushed
my mound against his hand to increase the lovely
sensation he was giving me.

'Rub harder, please,' I gasped as the fire between
my legs became hotter and hotter.

'Your wish is my command,' he grinned as he
jabbed two fingers into my sopping crack, his long
fingers groping inside my cunt until I yelped as he
found that incredibly sensitive spot at the bottom of my
quim. I quivered all over as he continued to finger-
fuck me, and I thought I would go out of my mind
when he found my clitty and began to make circles
around it with his thumb. The seat of the compartment
was now wet and slippery from my pussy juices and
my hips were jerking up and down, pushing wildly
against his hand.

Then he propped my legs up on his shoulders and
pushed up my skirt as he moved his head forward and
blew his warm breath on my soaking cunt, his lips
barely brushing my pouting love lips. Sweetie-pie, I
just cannot describe the excitement I felt as his tongue
now flicked along the edges of my slit. I let him go on
until I simply could not stand it any more and I wound

*my fingers through his curly dark hair and pushed his head away.*

*'I don't want to come yet, I want this to last,' I explained and I reached out and grabbed hold of Pete's stiff prick which was making a huge bulge in the front of his trousers. He hauled himself up and threw off his jacket and pulled down his trousers and pants before sitting down next to me. I clasped his naked cock in my hand and it felt so hard and so hot that without further ado I bent down and sucked his shaft deep into my throat. Then I brought it out again and ran my tongue up and down the pulsating pole and around the head.*

*'Mount me now!' he gasped and I straddled his huge cock and rode it, bouncing up and down in glee. I suppose it was as well that this was a non-stop express into Euston for, quite honestly, if anyone had come into the compartment, I wouldn't have cared and I couldn't have stopped even if I'd have wanted to, I was on such a pinnacle of ecstasy as I slid up and down on Pete's gorgeous prick. My legs were spread and my thighs gleamed with my juices as I humped up and down on his throbbing stiffie, and my heart was thumping as I came in a sudden release, clamping my thighs together around his shaft as I came in a huge rush.*

*My spasms pushed Pete over the top and he came too with a terrific yell of joy, and slowly I came back to earth as we fell into each other's arms, screaming with laughter as we hugged each other and, to my surprise, I realised that I could still feel his hard, palpitating prick inside me.*

*What a wonderful cock he has! I swear that Pete Bailey is hung like a horse! He pulled me up and flipped me over on my hands and knees and then he* pulled up my skirt and I turned my head round to see him grasp his throbbing tool and give it a loving shake.

'God! I can't take that huge cock up my bum!' I wailed but he said soothingly: 'Don't worry, my love, I just want to fuck you doggie-style,' as he sheathed his shaft between my bum cheeks and rolled up my jumper to cup my breasts in his hands. He teased me with his proud prick, letting his helmet just poke between my pussy lips and pushing it in just an inch before pulling out again. But then he began to push in a little more, then out, then back in and each time his enormous cock crept in a little deeper.

'Fuck me, Pete!' I cried out as his shaft slewed in to the hilt, and he began ramming in and out of my love box, building up a steady rhythm and making my cunny almost ache with delight until he finally spunked inside me and I came again just as he jetted a tremendous spray of creamy jism inside my tingling cunt and he collapsed down on me in a sweaty, spunky heap just as the train slowed down almost ot a standstill as we passed through Crewe station. I looked up and caught the eye of a porter on the platform and could not help laughing at the slack-jawed expression of amazement on his face as our carriage rolled slowly past him.

Well, that's the good news – the not so good news is that Pete is now away up in Scotland climbing in the Highlands with his brother Michael, and so I'll be all alone for the next ten days.

But it's not simply because Pete is away that I miss waking up beside you, Denise, moving the quilt so I can see the gentle curves of our soft bodies, both naked except for our tiny panties, being caressed by the dawn sunshine. We've been so busy with our boyfriends that it must be at least a month since we made love in the morning, which we used to do so regularly until

# A Very Naughty Night

Murray and Peter came on the scene.

Do you remember the last time we pleasured each other on the day before you left for Falmington? Wasn't it wonderful when your eyes fluttered open and I opened my arms and we kissed with such urgent passion, our questing tongues exploring and touching, our proud, thrusting breasts meeting and squeezing together, jutting nipple brushing against jutting nipple in tingles of sheer ecstasy as we stretched out our legs and let our toes stroke each other's smooth legs . . .

Then I hauled myself up and knelt between your legs and kissed that wispy stripe of hair which begins at your navel and trails down your tummy before widening and disappearing below the waistband of your panties. You purred with pleasure as I flicked my tongue over the delicate fuzz and worked my way downwards, swirling the tip of my tongue all round your belly button and down over the bulge of your panty-covered mound.

I'll never forget how you moaned with delight when I grasped the elastic edge of your panties with my teeth and tugged it down, and you lifted your chubby little bum off the sheet to assist me as I manoeuvered them down below your thighs and revealed all the glories of your sweet, hairy bush. Just thinking about your lovely pouting pussy lips is making me damp between my legs, and as I'm writing this I'm sliding the fingers of my left hand inside my knickers to fondle my moist crack.

I remember how I blew gently into your silky curls, brushing my cheek over your moistening slit and lightly nuzzling my lips against your stiffening clitty. 'M'mm, you'll make me come if you're not careful,' you murmured as my tongue burrowed inside your juicy cunny.

177

'Oh yes, yes, Jenny, don't stop, please, oh please!' *you cried out as I drew back for a moment to twirl my tongue over the hard nub of your clitty and felt the waves of my caress ripple through you. How I loved playing with your pussy, teasing around the edges, sucking open-mouthed and rolling the long love lips inside my mouth before plunging my tongue deep inside your sticky honeypot.*

'Woooh! Woooh!' *you shrieked as I worked my tongue till my jaw was aching, but I brought you off and lapped up your musky love juice whilst you continued to yell until your climax subsided. It was just as well that Mr Moser in the flat downstairs was away or he might have come charging upstairs to find out if someone was being attacked!*

*Ah well, so much for a lovely ride down memory lane. Write soon, darling, and tell me all your news.*

*Love,*
*Jenny*

Denise lay down the letter and lay back on her bed, pressing her warm cheek against the cool cotton of the pillow-case as she stretched her supple arms and legs as far as they would go, breathing deeply as she let her mind and body slide into the throes of an irresistible sexual reverie which held her in a delicious enveloping thrall.

With a sigh, Denise gave herself up to the powerful sensations which seeped through her and she started to caress her heaving breasts with trembling fingers, tweaking her large rubbery nipples between her fingers until they stood up stiff and erect. Then closing her eyes she parted her shapely thighs and gently ran her fingertips along the outer folds of her tingling pussy, stroking the soft flesh until she was gasping with joy and then with a thrill of sensual anticipation, she tenderly parted her yielding love lips and slowly inserted two fingers deep inside her juicy pussy, stimulating the walls of her love channel which contracted delightfully around them whilst with her thumb she rubbed the hard nub of her swollen clitty.

She began to pant, open-mouthed and her mind filled with erotic images of Jenny's delicious nude body, her firm, bouncy breasts, her silky blonde pussy through which her pink pussy lips peeked through so cheekily, and how she loved nothing better than for Denise to jab her long fingers inside her dripping honeypot, probing her wet, pulsating cunt.

Her breathing became more and more urgent as these potent pictures became more and more distinct, and with one hand she squeezed her jutting titties and with the other she slid her fingers in and out of her soaking quim, her head now rolling from side to side in an ecstasy of lust, her glossy hair spilling across her face.

Denise's body was now awash with desire as, aware of her rapidly approaching climax, she bent her knees and tensed her buttocks as she prodded her fingers in and out of her quivering cunny. But the lewd mental images of Jenny now changed to the last fleeting encounter she had exchanged with Murray Lupowitz on this very bed. Before he had left to return to his own hotel, she had murmured to him: 'There might not be time to make love, but please finger-fuck me before you go.'

She panted heavily as she saw herself raise her bottom off the bed to enable Murray to tug down her panties, and she had pulled up her skirt and opened her legs to reveal her fleshy pink love lips. She had been so wet that three of Murray's fingers had slid easily into her sopping slit and straight away he had set up a well-paced rhythm as they had kissed, working his fingers in and out, slowly at first and then faster and faster, whilst with his other hand he had tweaked her tawny nipples, rubbing them up to rosy little stalks as her body had jerked up and down in delight.

'A-a-h-r-e! A-a-h-r-e!' she gasped as she relaxed whilst the blissful, enveloping waves of her orgasm flowed out from her groin to fill every inch of her quivering body, pulsing over and over again with the unparalleled, delicious vibrance of sexual fulfilment.

When the delicious sensations of her climax finally died away, Denise lay silently on her bed, physically sated, and yet somehow she was far from being satisfied. The potent fire of sensual need remained as strong as ever inside her, despite the very real pleasure which had been afforded her by her sensual imagination and sensitive fingers. She reached out for the telephone to call Murray and beg him to come over immediately and spend the rest of the night with her.

Fortunately for Murray, Denise looked at her watch and when she saw that it was now well after midnight, she decided that Murray would either still be at the party at the College or he was more probably fast asleep in his room and it would be unreasonable to wake him up. And in any case, she should get in a good night's sleep because Mr Teplin often asked one of his students to read their essays out loud in class and she would need to be at her brightest in case he chose her, for afterwards there would be a general discussion on the student reader's dissertation.

In fact, Murray Lupowitz was indeed tucked up in bed at the Langham Park Hotel, but surprisingly he could not fall asleep, even after his strenuous sexual exertions with Lucy Gunther and Jacqui Burgess. 'I'm overtired, that's the trouble,' he muttered as he stretched out his arm and switched on the bedside light.

'I'll see if Fred the night porter can rustle up a Scotch

for me', he said to himself as he picked up the telephone and dialled the necessary extension, and he pricked up his ears when he heard a fresh young female voice answer: 'Night Porter, can I help you?'

'Hi there, this is room thirty-seven here, but that doesn't sound like old Fred to me.'

There was a little giggle and the voice replied: 'It is you, isn't it, Mr Lupowitz? I recognise your voice but do you recognise mine? Of course, you're right, I'm not old Fred, he reported in sick this afternoon and three of the girls are taking shifts to cover for him.'

A furrow appeared on Murray's brow as he tried to think to whom this mystery voice might belong. He suddenly snapped his fingers and said: 'It's Molly, isn't it? My God, you'll be in no fit state to serve breakfast in the morning if you don't get to bed soon.'

'It's my day off tomorrow so I don't have to get up at the crack of dawn, thank goodness,' she replied pertly. 'Now, what can I do for you?'

'I'd better not give you a truthful reply to that question,' said Murray with a chuckle as a mental picture formed in his mind of the big, bouncy breasts of the young waitress jiggling up and down as she walked across the dining-room. 'But instead I'll ask you if it's possible for someone to bring up a double Scotch with some ice to my room?'

'I'll do it myself, Mr Lupowitz. Marilyn's just arrived to take over from me. I'll be with you in just a couple of minutes,' she promised and Molly was as good as her word for, after putting down the telephone, Murray only had time to slip on a dressing gown and go to the bathroom for a pee before he heard the noise of the lift which was almost opposite his door.

Seconds later there was a knock on the door and he padded across the room and opened it. Sure enough, with a tray in her hands was the perky little red-headed girl who had been waiting at his table since he arrived at the Langham Park.

'Hello, Mr Lupowitz,' she said cheerfully as she came in, and he shut the door behind her. 'We've only got a cupboard of miniature bottles as the bar's closed, but as you wanted a double, I've brought up two for you and the ice is in the bowl. Would you just like to sign the bill for me?'

'Thanks, Molly,' he said, scrawling his name on the proferred piece of paper. 'I don't really need two bottles, but I've a great idea – why don't you help me polish them off? Hold on and I'll bring in another glass from the bathroom.'

'That's very nice of you, Mr Lupowitz, I won't say no,' she said and he interrupted her, saying: 'Only one condition. Stop with all this Mr Lupowitz business, the name is Murray.'

'Okay Mr – I mean, Murray,' she said as he strode into the bathroom to collect an extra glass. 'Have you been out tonight or did you have a boring evening watching the television?'

'I was at a great party up at the College,' he replied as he came back with the glass which he put on the tray. 'And I've been in for about half an hour, but for some reason I just can't seem to get to sleep.'

'I'm not tired either, which is funny because I worked till tea-time and I've been on this night duty since eight o'clock,' she said, nodding as he held a spoon with ice-cubes over her glass. 'And in between I didn't get much rest either!'

Murray poured the drinks and they clinked their glasses together. 'Cheers, Molly,' he said and they gulped down generous draughts of the fiery spirit. 'Go out to see your boyfriend, did you?' he added teasingly.

She shook her head. 'No, I split up with my fella last

month. But I did have a great time with a guy this afternoon. You know that Shane Hammond is starring at the Queen's on Sunday week?'

'Sure, I've seen him a few times on television.'

'Yes, so have I,' said Molly, accepting Murray's invitation to sit with him on his bed. 'But my friend Julie and I are much more interested in the singer Chris Kirby who's also on the bill.'

Murray thought for a moment. 'Oh yes, the tall young blond guy, I've seen him on TV as well, haven't I? He had a hit with, what was the name of the record, oh yeah, *My Kind of Luck*. You fancy Chris, do you?'

'Not half. The other night my friend Julie and I waited for half an hour outside the stage door after the show, but he must have left through another exit to escape the fans. There must have been at least fifty girls there waiting for him.'

'Lucky man,' commented Murray as he opened the second bottle of Scotch and poured it into their glasses. 'So what did you do? Leave a note for Chris asking for an autograph with the doorman? That's usually the best way at least to get a signed photograph.'

'Well, that's exactly what I did, only I didn't get a photograph but I did get a letter from his manager, a guy named Charlie Haynes, inviting me to come and see him at the theatre this afternoon at four o'clock.

'I was working in the dining-room till half past three so I didn't have time to change, so I had to go along in my uniform, you know, the white blouse and black skirt. Anyhow, I got to the theatre and showed the letter to the commissionaire and he took me to see Charlie Haynes in one of the offices on the mezzanine floor between the stalls and the circle.

'Charlie turned out to be a smart guy of about thirty and he asked me whether I was a really keen fan of Chris, because he was looking for someone to help him start up a Falmington branch of the Chris Kirby Fan Club. It wouldn't involve much work except to have my photograph taken with Chris as he would look after all the paperwork, collecting the subscriptions, sending out a newsletter and photographs, all that kind of thing.

' "So are you interested, Molly?" he asked me and of course I replied: "I should say so, when can we start?"

## TO BE CONTINUED IN SUMMER SCHOOL 2: ALL-NIGHT GIRLS